# Saige

by Jessie Haas

★ American Girl®

*For Jo McNeil.*
*Love you, miss you.*

Published by American Girl Publishing
Copyright © 2013 American Girl

Questions or comments? Call 1-800-845-0005, visit **americangirl.com**, or write to
Customer Service, American Girl, 8400 Fairway Place, Middleton, WI 53562-0497.

Printed in China
13  14  15  16  17  18  19  20  LEO  16  15  14  13  12  11  10

Illustrations by Sarah Davis

Special thanks to Beth Larsen, Executive Director of Art in the School, Albuquerque, NM;
Randy Cohen, Vice President of Research and Policy, Americans for the Arts;
Amy Robinson, Master Dog Trainer and Director of Country View Canines, Oregon, WI;
and Karla Dean at Country View Veterinary Service, Oregon, WI.

Photo credits, pp. 118–123: Barry Bland, Kitson Jazynka, and James Youells

Library of Congress Cataloging-in-Publication Data

Haas, Jessie.
Saige / by Jessie Haas ; [illustrations by Sarah Davis].
p. cm.
Summary: Upset that her New Mexico school can only afford music and art teachers in
alternate years, fourth-grader Saige works with her grandmother, Mimi, to plan a fund-
raiser, but when Mimi has an accident, Saige relies on new friend Gabi to help.
ISBN 978-1-60958-166-4 (pbk. : alk. paper) —ISBN 978-1-60958-167-1 (hardcover : alk. paper)
[1. Fund raising—Fiction. 2. Arts—Fiction. 3. Schools—Fiction. 4. Horses—Fiction. 5. Trick
riding—Fiction. 6. Friendship—Fiction. 7. Family life—New Mexico—Fiction. 8. New
Mexico—Fiction.] I. Davis, Sarah, 1971–, ill. II. Title.
PZ7.H1129Sai 2013      [Fic] —dc23      2012034016

# Contents

"Saige! Hurry!" Mom called from the front step.

"Sam! Hurry!" I echoed from halfway up the street. I tugged on the leash, but my dog, Sam, a shaggy black-and-white Border collie mix, ignored me. He was too busy sniffing a telephone pole, reading the message left by some other dog. You can't hurry that.

I turned in a circle, seeing tan stucco houses, the color of adobe. A few tall cottonwood trees stood behind them. The dry brown lawns were just starting to green up from the August rains. Off to the east, the Sandia Mountains were bluish gray under the rising sun, and everything else was dust-colored—unless you looked up.

I did, at the huge, deep, brilliant blue sky. New Mexico has so much sky, it makes everything else seem tiny. A yellow hot-air balloon drifted overhead, the perfect accent.

Albuquerque is the hot-air balloon capital of the world. We're known for the Albuquerque International Balloon Fiesta, which happens every year in October. Hundreds of balloons participate, and thousands of people watch. But balloons fly here nearly all year, especially in the mornings. My dad flies one. He's a commercial airplane pilot and a certified balloon pilot—and fanatic.

"C'mon, Sam, let's go!" I urged, running for home with Sam racing alongside me. We burst into the kitchen just as the toast popped up.

Mom slathered a couple of pieces of toast with peanut butter and mesquite honey and dished out the eggs. Then we sat down together, just us two. Dad had left a couple of hours ago. He usually eats breakfast at the airport.

Mom propped her chin on one hand as she ate. Her springy red hair wasn't combed yet, and her eyelids hung heavy. Mornings aren't Mom's thing, but I felt sparkly and alive.

"First day of school," I told Sam as he parked himself next to my chair. His ears flattened. He knows lots of words, and "school" isn't a favorite. It means I'll be leaving the house soon.

"Looking forward to fourth grade?" Mom asked.

"Yes!" I answered, toast crumbs spraying. "I can't *wait* to see Tessa!"

"And learn?" Mom suggested. She teaches math at the university, so learning is big for her. I took a bite of my eggs so that I didn't have to answer. I do like learning, but sometimes school can make even interesting things seem boring. There's a good part, though—Miss Fane's art class. Remembering that, I chewed faster.

Sam stared at me with his power gaze, the one that's supposed to put sheep into an obedient trance. *Toast,* he commanded silently. *Toast.* I broke off a corner and tossed it to him. *Gulp.* The gaze immediately resumed.

Sam and I shared the last bite of toast, and then I went to brush my teeth. I glanced at my hair in the mirror. It's long and auburn, and I'd done it in a loose side braid. It looked good, I thought, and showed off the silver earrings Mom had given me.

After pulling on my red knit sweater, I was fed and dressed—almost ready for school. Now, *supplies.* I unzipped the side pocket of my backpack and turned to my art table.

Colored pencils. Did I need my colored pencils?

Sure. You never know when you're going to need some yellow or turquoise in your life.

Double-ended felt-tipped brush-pen?

Well, duh! It *is* the best drawing implement on the planet.

Except for a nice sharp No. 2 pencil. Better

grab a couple of those, and my tiny metal pencil sharpener.

"Saige! Bus!" my mom called.

The bus roared past the house. Not a problem— I don't ride the bus, but it's my signal to get moving. I struggled to close the side pocket of my backpack. Maybe I'd gone overboard with the pens and pencils, but you can never have too many things to draw with, right?

I heaved the backpack onto my shoulders and plunged through the kitchen, planting a flying kiss on Mom's cheek—so fast that it was almost a head-butt. Then I gave Sam's head a quick pat. "See you this afternoon," I promised him.

"Have fun!" Mom called to my back. "Learn a lot—"

The door banged shut behind me. I peeled down our front path. The morning air was nice and cool, but that wouldn't last long today. School starts in mid-August in Albuquerque, and New Mexican summers are *hot*.

The bus had stopped down the street, at the house where I'd seen a moving van this past weekend. A family with kids must have moved in. Little kids? Big kids? Boys? Girls?

Whoever they were, they were already on the bus. It pulled away as I turned down Mesa Road and poured on the speed, my pack slapping heavily against my back. This wasn't the best-ever outfit for running. My feet were slipping in my new red sandals, and I could feel my braid loosening.

I sprinted past the yard with the desert landscaping, past the big backyard with the burros. I rounded the next corner and ran across the soccer field. Up ahead, the bus pulled into the school driveway. I reached the bus door, panting, as the first kid got off.

In a moment Tessa came down the steps. She wore a green T-shirt with a treble clef on the front—like a backward S with a line down the middle. Her wavy blonde hair spilled onto her shoulders, and she was wearing her dangly earrings that I love. They're made of tiny beads that jingle when she turns her head or laughs.

"Hi!" I said, grinning broadly.

"Saige!" Tessa said back, smiling our special smile—pressing her lips together and squeezing her eyes almost shut. I invented the smile, imitating how a cat beams. Tessa has wide cheekbones, and her short nose tips up a little. When she beams, she really does

5

look like a Persian cat.

"How was music camp?" I asked.

"It was *awesome!*" she declared. "We sang for four hours a day! I learned a ton about breath control and how to project my voice into my mask . . ."

There was more, but I didn't understand half of it—I mean, *really* didn't understand. It was like she was speaking another language.

"Where are the new kids?" I asked, changing the subject. "I saw the bus stop at the house on our street that just sold."

Tessa pointed at the sidewalk ahead. A skinny dark-haired girl walked all alone toward the front doors of the school. Her backpack wasn't especially big, but it looked like it was weighing her down.

Tessa and I followed the new girl through the doors and into the hallway. Blank beige walls and lockers stretched as far as the eye could see. Last year the walls were lined with our artwork: cactus drawings; foil pierced to look like Spanish tinwork; paintings of the brilliant pink Sandia Mountains at sunset; and balloons, balloons, balloons. The art went home with us at the end of last year and left the walls bare, an empty desert.

"I can't wait till the new artwork starts to go

up," I said, quickening my step.

Tessa gave me a pitying look. "Saige, don't be such a space cadet," she teased. "We don't have art this year. We have music!"

I stared at her, suddenly feeling crushed. How could I have forgotten something this bad, even for a minute? In Albuquerque, public elementary schools have an art teacher one year and a music teacher the next—never both at the same time. The school system can't afford it.

"Sorry," Tessa said, giving me a quick cat smile. "But does it really matter? You paint every afternoon with Mimi. Anyway, we *do* get to have music."

Mimi is my grandma. Her real name is Miriam, but everyone calls her "Mimi," and she's a pretty well-known artist in our community. Tessa was right: I do paint with my artist-grandmother almost every day. And we do get music this year, and music is fun.

But my backpack was full of drawing pencils and pens.

And I had new drawings to show Miss Fane, the art teacher.

And there's nothing about school that I love as much as art. I love being a star, the one who can draw horses that really *look* like horses. I love learning new techniques—and following my own creative ideas, too.

Tessa looked miffed. "Well, *I'm* happy about music class," she said.

Tessa is my best friend, so I should have been happy for her. She loves music the way that I love art. I should have said, "Yay! Music!"

But I couldn't make myself feel happy, even for Tessa, and I certainly couldn't make myself smile. I'd gone from sparkly to depressed in two seconds flat.

Ahead of us, the new girl had stopped walking and was glancing back at us. Her skin was the color of coffee with lots of milk, her eyes wide and dark.

"Excuse me," she said. "Did you just say we don't get *art* this year?"

Tessa and I nodded.

The girl's eyes filled with tears. "We didn't have it *last* year at my old school," she said softly.

I had to look away from her in case I started to cry, too. That meant looking at the blank wall. Usually there's nothing I love more than a blank canvas or an empty sheet of white paper, waiting for me to do something wonderful to it.

But these walls weren't like that. They were just dull, and without art, they were probably going to stay that way. I couldn't stand looking at them a second longer.

I turned back toward the new girl. "What's your name?" I asked.

"Gabi Peña," she said shyly. "I'm in fourth grade—Mrs. Applegate's room."

"Us, too!" Tessa said. "We'll show you where it is. Where are you from?"

Gabi and her family had moved from the South Valley, she told us as we walked. She had a four-year-old brother and a baby sister.

"Do you have any pets?" I asked.

Gabi's eyes filled with tears again. "Our dog died last month," she said sadly. "Mom doesn't want to get another one till we're settled in."

I felt terrible for bringing up another upsetting topic. I was glad when Gabi blinked back her tears and pinned on a braver look. "You have a dog, right?" she asked. "I saw you walking him last night."

I told Gabi about Sam as we walked together into our new homeroom. It was set up with big tables, four chairs at each. A few kids were there already, including Dylan Patterson at the front table.

Dylan is tall and brown-haired, and I noticed that she was wearing the same green music-camp shirt that Tessa was wearing.

"Over here, Tessa!" Dylan called. "I got us a table."

*Us?* When did Dylan and Tessa become "us"? Tessa and *I* were us.

"Saige, you can sit with us, too," said Dylan, pointing toward another chair at the table. I suddenly remembered how bossy she could be.

I was going to keep walking, but Tessa seemed to be going along with all of this. "C'mon, Gabi," said Tessa. "We can sit at the same table." She plopped down beside Dylan, and they both started talking about music.

"That last lesson was the best," Dylan said. "Making the inside of your mouth like a cathedral! And rubber corks in the hinge of your jaw—"

"I know," Tessa interrupted, nodding her head vigorously as if what Dylan had said made perfect sense.

For a second I felt a pinch of jealousy. Dylan's okay, but she isn't one of *us*. There are only *two* of *us*.

Tessa and Dylan were acting like best buddies, though. Clearly Tessa'd had a great time at music camp, and Dylan had shared it with her.

But summer was over now. We were back

in school, and Tessa and I would have as much fun together as we always did—well, *almost* as much fun. It was still hard to think about a year without art.

Mrs. Applegate took attendance and then got started with our first subject, history.

Right away I could tell that fourth grade was going to be harder than third. There would be more homework, Mrs. Applegate told us, and we'd be doing research reports. She didn't call them "hard." She called them "more sophisticated." I knew what that meant, though.

At lunch, Tessa told me more—lots more— about what she had learned at music camp. "Do you know how much practice it takes to get really, really good at something?" she asked. *"Ten thousand hours!* To become a soloist or a virtuoso, it takes ten thousand hours of practice."

"Not that you're counting," I joked.

Tessa didn't laugh. "I *am* counting!" she said, glancing at Dylan. "Dylan and I made a pact. We've already put in five hours each since camp ended."

"Only nine thousand, nine hundred and ninety-five hours to go," I said.

It was a good line—and good math—but it was a horrifying idea. If Tessa really believed this, when was she going to find any time to have fun with me? And without art class, how was I going to get ten thousand hours doing what *I* loved? I couldn't wait for the school day to end so that I could take my troubles to Mimi.

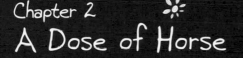
My grandmother lives out where neighborhoods give way to little *ranchitas* and orchards. It's almost the last stop on the school-bus route.

I walked up the driveway under white, baking sunlight and stepped under the huge old cottonwood trees into a different world. It was cooler here. Green and yellow light filtered through shifting layers of leaves. From high above me, I heard birdsong. Beneath the trees, glossy black chickens with chalk-white faces scratched in the dirt, chortling and shaking their bright red combs.

"Hello!" I called toward the house. Mimi's dog, Rembrandt, woofed in answer. His voice sounds just like Sam's, because they're brothers, two black-and-white Border collie mixes.

A moment later Mimi appeared at the doorway of the adobe ranch house, sweeping a wide-brimmed hat off her head. Her smile was a slice of white in her tanned face. She wore jeans and rawhide chaps—she must have been working a horse. "Good!" she said. That's what Mimi always says when she sees me: Good!

"*Not* good," I said. "We don't have *art* this year!"

"Is that right?" Mimi asked, twisting her thick

gray hair up into a bun. She glanced under her
arm at me. "Did we know that was coming? I can't
remember."

"I guess I knew," I admitted, "but I forgot."

Mimi took off her glasses and wiped away the
dust. "Well, let's solve this over a cold glass of lemonade, shall we?" she said, waving me inside.

I followed her into the cool house. In the dim
light, the large paintings and brilliant fabrics draping
the furniture almost glowed. Mimi's house was so
interesting and colorful, the exact opposite of school.

Mimi got out two heavy glasses, filled them
from the jug in the refrigerator, and led the way to the
studio. It was the first time I'd been in the studio in
almost three weeks, but nothing had changed. Two
easels faced the big window that looked out over the
horse pasture and the Sandia Mountains. Adjustable
lamps leaned over the drafting table, as if peeking at
the artwork and the collection of jars bristling with
brushes. And in the corner was the comfy old sofa,
covered with red, gray, and black Navajo saddle
blankets.

The pasture and mountains beyond the
window were where things changed. The horses
might be out there, or they might not. The Sandias

might be bluish gray, like this morning, or cool pink, like this afternoon, or that astonishingly vivid watermelon pink that gives them their name. *Sandia* means watermelon.

Mimi's easel held a blank canvas with photos of her horses pinned above it. There was light-gray Picasso, bay Georgia, the little brown yearling named Jackson, big-bellied Mama Frida, dappled Laurel, and palomino Berthe. All of Mimi's animals are named after artists, including Rembrandt—and my dog, Sam, too. He's named after Sam Savitt, who is famous for his horse paintings and who also wrote my favorite how-to art book.

As I sipped my lemonade, I heard a bark and the scrabble of claws on the floor. A fluffy kitten raced into the studio half an inch ahead of Rembrandt. She leaped onto the sofa next to me and arched her back at him.

"When did you get a kitten?" I asked as Rembrandt crouched, staring at the kitten the way Sam had stared at my toast.

Mimi said, "Somebody dumped her off about a week ago. I heard a car drive off, and fifteen minutes later she was on the doorstep. Rembrandt likes her, but the last thing I need in the studio is a kitten, knocking things down and getting hair on the paintings."

The kitten scrambled onto the sofa back and beamed at me, purring. She looked just like Tessa, except Tessa doesn't have a fuzzy face, half white and half gray, divided by a straight line down the middle of her nose.

"She's so cute!" I exclaimed, scratching the kitten's head.

When I looked up, Mimi was watching me thoughtfully.

"So, no art this year," she said. "Do you want to try to do something about it?"

I stared at Mimi. *Do* something—other than just moping? "Like what?" I asked.

"Get the PTA to help with the arts fiesta," Mimi said promptly.

Mimi and her Oil Painters Society were planning a neighborhood fiesta to raise money for arts in the community. The paintings on our easels were going into the silent auction, if we finished them in time, and I'd agreed to teach kids how to draw horses at the fiesta. So I was helping already, but Mimi seemed to think we could do more—which was pretty typical of her.

# A Dose of Horse

Mimi said, "Maybe we could have volunteers teach after-school art classes during the off years, when your school doesn't have an art teacher. We would need supplies, and we'd probably need to pay a regular teacher or two to stay and supervise. The money we raise can help with that, but if the PTA joins us, we can raise *more* money."

"When would we start having classes?" I asked, suddenly feeling excited. "And who's going to teach?"

"Whoa, slow down," Mimi said. "We have to raise the money first. We have a barbecue arranged for the fiesta, but no bake sale yet. That would be a good project for the PTA to take on. Your mom's a member, right? Maybe you can talk to her about it."

"O . . . kay," I sighed, feeling deflated again. Bake sales are all right, but not nearly as much fun as art class.

Mimi smiled at me. "I know, all this just to get an art class," she said. "But getting where you want to go takes time and effort."

I nodded, thinking of Tessa. "Ten thousand hours," I said. When Mimi raised her eyebrows questioningly, I explained.

"Tessa is exactly right!" said Mimi. "Putting

in practice time is just as important as having talent.
Sounds as if Tessa learned and grew a lot at music
camp. I'm glad for her."

A picture of Tessa and Dylan in their matching
shirts flashed through my mind. "Me, too," I said,
trying to mean it.

Mimi must have heard the uncertainty in my
voice. "You need a dose of horse," she said, "and then
we'll get to work painting."

I followed her out to the shady three-sided
shed where the horses were sheltered from the heat
of the day. When I stepped in among them, Picasso
turned his head toward me politely.

Mimi's horses are Spanish Barbs, an ancient
strain of horse brought to America by the Spanish
*conquistadors*, soldiers and explorers from the 1500s.
Spanish Barbs are rare—there are fewer than a
thousand of them left. But Mimi owns five and is
doing all she can to help preserve Spanish Barbs.

Picasso seems to know he comes from noble
blood and always acts like the perfect gentleman. He
blew his warm, sweet breath over my face, making
my skin prickle. His almond-shaped eyes looked wise
and kind.

I reached up under Picasso's long white mane

and gave him a scratch.

"Hey, he's sweaty!" I said, glancing at his sides. Picasso is white, flecked all over with dark speckles. Today the hair on his back was rough and damp. "You were riding him?" I asked. Usually Mimi rides the younger horses, who are all still in training.

Mimi said, "Picasso and I are coming out of retirement for the fiesta. We're going to dust off some of our old rodeo tricks."

I raised my eyebrows. Mimi is a young-looking and young-acting grandmother, but she's over sixty, and Picasso is twenty-seven, which is pretty old for a horse. When they were younger, Mimi did trick riding on him. I'd seen pictures of Picasso galloping around an arena while Mimi stood in the saddle or leaned down to pick a handkerchief off the ground. There's even a picture of her jumping him, bareback and without a bridle, through a flaming hoop.

"*Really?* The flaming hoop and everything?" I asked.

Mimi shook her head regretfully. "We'll do something a lot less dangerous," she explained. "We're not quite the athletes we used to be. There's a parade, too. Do you want to lead the parade on Picasso?"

"*Lead* the parade?" That sounded scary, to be out there in front of the crowd all by myself.

"Picasso is the most experienced parade horse around here," Mimi said. "Don't you think he belongs in the lead?"

I looked deep into Picasso's eyes. There's an old Spanish saying that Barbs are both "fire and feather." That's Picasso. He's high-spirited and hot-blooded, yet as easy to handle as a feather. I've ridden him since I was very small, and he takes care of me. Plus he's beautiful. If I rode him in the parade, people wouldn't be looking at me. They'd be looking at Picasso.

"I'd like that," I answered.

Mimi smiled. "Good! He'd like it too," she said, patting Picasso's side. "You'll need to start riding a few afternoons a week so that you both get into shape. But let's not get too far ahead of ourselves. First, I'd like to get back to the studio and start that painting. I don't paint as much when you're not around, Saige. Did you know that?"

"You don't sit *still* long enough," I said. Mimi is always doing something with horses, or gardening, or fixing fences on the ranch—always moving, and moving *fast*. But during the school year, I come to Mimi's most afternoons. Then Mimi sits, and we both get a lot of painting done.

Back in the studio, I looked at the painting I'd left on the easel three weeks ago. It was a portrait of Picasso, and I didn't like it anymore. It looked crude to me, babyish. I was sure I could do better.

*Should I start over? Or try to fix it?* I wondered. That's the cool thing about painting with oils. A lot of times you can cover up mistakes. I sat and stared. What did I *like* about the painting?

The eyes. Somehow I had gotten that Picasso expression, the wise yet fiery look. *So, keep the eyes,* I told myself. *And the ears, and the nose. And the neck.*

So what exactly was wrong with this picture?

*The jaw,* I decided. I'd messed up the perspective, so Picasso's jowl seemed to flare out. I could hide that by deepening the shadow on his neck. I squeezed some paint onto my palette and stepped close to the painting again.

Later—fifteen minutes? An hour?—I heard a sigh from Mimi. I surfaced from my painting trance, put my palette down, and walked over to see what she was doing.

I'd been expecting Mimi's painting to be naturalistic, to look like horses really look. Mimi does that so well, people sometimes mistake her horse paintings for photographs.

But this painting was pink, the deep ruby-hued pink of the Sandia Mountains at sunset. The horses were closely grouped together, so their ears, necks, backs, and rumps made one continuous line, like . . . I looked out the window.

Like the mountains. "Mountain horses!" I declared.

"Yes, I might just call it that," Mimi said, sounding pleased.

"It's *amazing*," I said. It was hard to pull my gaze away from the painting.

Mimi stood up and walked to my easel. "Hmm," she said thoughtfully.

"There's too much shadow on the neck, right?" I asked.

"How would you fix that?" Mimi asked.

"Um, I could darken the other shadows, I guess," I said, reaching for my palette again.

At that moment, Rembrandt barked, which meant my dad was here. I looked around for my backpack.

Dad walked in, still looking crisp in his pilot's uniform. He's short and wiry, just like Mimi. "Hi, Ma!

Hi, Saige!" he called to us. "How was your day?"

"Great!" I said and then laughed. I wouldn't have said that two hours earlier, but the lost sparkle had come back to the day. School hadn't started the way I'd hoped, but school wasn't everything. And anyway, Mimi and I already had a plan to make it better.

# Chapter 3
## Singing Off-Key

I shared Mimi's fund-raising idea with Mom over dinner. "I think it's a great idea," she said. "I was just reading about how students get better grades when schools devote enough time to the arts. It's worth fighting for."

Mom paused to scoop corn onto my plate and then said, "Why don't you write the PTA a letter and get classmates to sign it? I can bring it to the meeting next week. Make sure to ask who wants to help sell cookies at the fiesta!"

"I'll donate balloon rides," Dad volunteered. He's always looking for more reasons to fly his balloon.

"Yes! You could even make it a raffle," Mom suggested. "Sell tickets, and the winner gets to go up with you in a mass ascension during Balloon Fiesta."

"Good idea. I'll need a ticket booth . . ." Dad said, staring into space. He may be a detail-focused airline pilot by day, but he *is* Mimi's son, so he has his artistic side. He came out of his daydream long enough to turn to me and say, "I might need some help, Saige."

"Sure!" I felt good about all of this. I'd gotten things rolling, and tomorrow I'd get Tessa to help me write the letter. She's better with words than I am.

Then sometime soon, we'd have after-school art classes.

⁂

The next morning I was outside walking Sam, listening to distant dogs barking at distant hot-air balloons, when Gabi's front door opened.

"Hi," Gabi said, coming down the walk. "May I say hello to your dog?"

"Sure," I said, giving Sam the "sit" command.

Gabi crouched down beside Sam. She didn't pat him on the head or stare into his face, as most people do when they greet a dog. She didn't look at him at all. She turned her head toward the mountains and held out her clenched fist so that Sam could smell it. He checked it out and then looked up at her face. Only then did she look down.

"Hello, Sam. What beautiful eyes!" she said soothingly.

Sam leaned against her leg, something he usually does only with family. He was already devoted to her.

"Wow," I said. "You really understand dogs!"

Gabi nodded. "I taught our old dog to do tricks," she said, "like helping Mama pick up after the baby. I'd like to be a dog trainer when I grow up."

"Cool! My grandmother trains horses," I said.
"She has a horse she does tricks on." I told Gabi about
Picasso, and her eyes lit up, like Tessa's when she
talks about music.

"I go out to my aunt's ranch every summer,"
Gabi said. "We trained one of her horses to do tricks
this year. It was really fun."

"Wa . . ." I began. I was going to say, "Want to
come out and meet Picasso?" But going to Mimi's was
something I usually did with Tessa. I was hoping Tessa
would come out sometime this week, if she had time.
"Want to walk to school together?" I asked instead.

Gabi turned pink, suddenly seeming shy again.
"Okay," she said.

"Great!" I said, turning back toward my house.
"I'll come get you in about half an hour."

A short while later, we were walking to school
instead of running cross-lots the way I usually did.
I learned that Gabi had a best friend back in the South
Valley named Renata. They talked every night on the
phone, but Gabi wasn't sure they'd stay best friends
now that they couldn't see each other every day. Renata
was already planning a sleepover at someone else's
house.

I knew how Gabi felt. I was hoping that today

everything would go back to normal between me and Tessa. Maybe Tessa would be tired of the ten-thousand-hours thing, tired of Dylan, ready to help me write the PTA letter, and free to come out to Mimi's in the afternoon.

But when we walked into the classroom, Dylan and Tessa were already there making faces—their jaws hanging slackly and their eyes wide. They looked ridiculous, actually.

"We're pretending we have rubber corks at the hinges of our jaws," Tessa told me happily. "It helps you relax your mouth—"

"So it's as big as a cathedral," I snapped, louder than I meant to. "I know!"

Tessa closed her mouth, and I caught a glimpse of hurt in her eyes. I instantly wished I could take back my words, but class was starting, and there was no more time to talk.

At lunch, I tried to make things better by telling Tessa all about the art fiesta. "I have this letter to write to the PTA," I explained. "Could you help me with it?"

Tessa shook her head. "Dylan and I are

doing our math homework right after we eat," she said. "We're going to try to get our homework done during the day so that we have more time for lessons and practice after school."

Dylan tapped Tessa's shoulder, trying to get her attention, but I pressed on. "Could you help me tomorrow, maybe after school?" I asked.

Tessa looked torn. "Tomorrow I have a voice lesson," she said, "and Thursday there's piano."

"What about tonight?" I asked. "Could you come out to Mimi's?"

I saw Tessa and Dylan exchange a glance. Did she need Dylan's permission now before she made any decisions?

Apparently so. Dylan gave Tessa one of those looks that means *You know what you have to do,* and Tessa raised her hands apologetically. "I have to practice, Saige," she said.

"Well, when *will* we get together?" I asked. Suddenly things were looking completely hopeless.

"I don't know," Tessa said. She looked a little frustrated, too. Then her face brightened. "I know! Maybe we can go to a movie Friday night. Do you want to?"

I nodded. Friday night movies were somethi~

Tessa and I did a lot—at least last year.

"Okay, then," said Tessa. "I'll ask my parents."

Then she turned to Dylan to talk about—what else?—music. A teacher at camp had told Tessa that she had perfect pitch. If somebody struck a piano key, Tessa could identify the note and sing it.

Dylan wanted to test Tessa's pitch using a piano app on her cell phone. Sure enough, Tessa aced the test.

"Do it again!" said Dylan.

When Tessa got another perfect score, Dylan sighed admiringly. Then I saw Tessa give Dylan a playfully smug cat smile.

But that was *our* smile! Why was Tessa sharing it with Dylan? And weren't they supposed to be doing homework? That didn't look like homework to me.

"Tonight won't work anyway," I said to Tessa's back. "I forgot—Mimi and I will be riding." *That ought to get her!* Tessa loves horses. But she hardly noticed.

The person who did notice was Gabi, who listened at the edge of our group with shining eyes. She was dying to come out and meet the horses, I could tell. But she didn't ask about that. Instead she said, "I could help you with the letter, if you want."

I nodded, feeling confused. Tessa *always* helps me with writing things. Why did it feel as if everything was changing?

❧

When I arrived at the *ranchita*, Mimi had Picasso and Georgia, the beautiful four-year-old bay mare, saddled. After lemonade, we rode out—Mimi on Georgia and me on Picasso—across the hot pasture and into the Bosque, the woodland along the banks of the Rio Grande. It was cooler there and breezy. The river glittered in the spaces between the trees, and we heard ducks quacking.

Georgia pointed her ears toward the sound. This was her first time in the Bosque. She danced and sidestepped beside Picasso, startled by every shadow. Picasso glided along with his long-striding walk, ignoring the shadows—and ignoring Georgia, mostly. But when she seemed to be holding her breath, ready to explode, he reached out and nudged her shoulder. Georgia relaxed a bit, matching her stride to his.

Mimi and I smiled at each other and rode quietly, side by side, in the dappled shade. When she was on horseback, Mimi looked young. And on wise Picasso, I felt mature and seasoned, as if Mimi and

I were the same age, or as if age didn't really matter. What mattered was what people thought about and cared about, and in that way, Mimi and I were alike. So what if she was fifty years older than me?

On Thursday Mimi showed me her trick-riding routine for the fiesta. First she warmed up Picasso, circling the ring at a walk and a slow jog. When he was ready, she rode him over to the fence, reached forward, and slipped the bridle off Picasso's head. She handed it to me. "Now watch this," she said, grinning.

She picked up two pieces of red fabric from the fence rail. They were long rectangles of light, floaty cloth, streaked with flame-like orange and blue. She took one cloth in each hand, put both fists on her hips, and turned Picasso away from the fence, using just her knees to guide him.

Out in the middle of the ring, Mimi did something else. I couldn't see what it was, but Picasso changed. He held himself proudly, arched his neck, and began a powerful, slow prance around the ring. The flame-colored cloths rippled at his sides, tracing patterns in the air. It was beautiful.

Suddenly Mimi's loud cowboy whistle split the air, and Picasso burst into a gallop. Mimi raised her arms high above her head in a perfect V, and the cloths streamed wildly out behind her. Picasso circled the whole ring. Then Mimi guided him in a fast figure eight with her knees.

"*Que bonita!*" called Luis, Mimi's neighbor, as he approached the ring and leaned against the fence beside me. He's tall and sturdy and always wears black and silver. Today he wore a silver bracelet on his wrist and silver *conchos*—round disks threaded onto a leather string—on the band of his black cowboy hat. Luis is an artist like Mimi. He works with all kinds of metal.

"I come over for a dozen eggs, and I get a Wild West show," he said, smiling.

Leaning back in the saddle, Mimi brought Picasso to a fast, skidding stop and then walked him over to the fence. Picasso's nostrils flared red, and his sides heaved.

"What'd'ya think?" Mimi asked me with a grin.

"That was awesome!" I said, giving her a thumbs-up.

Just then Mom's car appeared at the end of the driveway. "See you tomorrow?" Mimi asked.

I shook my head. "Tomorrow I'm going home with Tessa," I said.

Mimi must have known just what that meant to me, because she answered with one word: "Good."

I used to know Tessa's room almost as well as my own, but when I walked in on Friday afternoon, I saw that it had changed. Music was everywhere—posters, books, a guitar, sheet music, and CDs.

"Wow, your room looks so different from . . . from the last time I saw it," I stammered. When *was* the last time I'd been there?

"Yeah, Dylan gave me some posters when we got back from music camp," said Tessa. "She has the same ones up in her room."

*Dylan* again. I tried not to grimace.

It was easy to smile, though, when Tessa's mom walked through the front door. She immediately gave me a hug. "Saige! Good to see you, sweetheart," she said. "Let me get out of these shoes, and we'll go get us some green-chile cheeseburgers."

I love Tessa's mom. And I loved my green-chile cheeseburger, going down the street to the theater, and sitting in the velvet-covered seats, sharing hot buttered popcorn with Tessa. We watched a dog movie, an adventure, and it was really bad. The scary parts made us laugh, the sad parts made us laugh, and the funny parts made us groan, they were so lame. But it all felt good. Finally, everything seemed back to normal.

On the ride home, Tessa started humming a cowboy song under her breath. I joined in, singing the words. Dad listens to old-time Western singers with scratchy, nasal voices, and Tessa and I like to imitate them. "I ride an old paint," I screeched, making my voice break on purpose. Tessa didn't join in, so I did just one verse and the chorus.

"Let's sing 'The Lone Prairie,'" suggested Tessa. She sang it pretty, her voice soft and pure. I started to sing it like one of Dad's faves, but as we passed under a streetlight, I saw Tessa frowning. *Better to play it straight,* I thought as I joined in. "These words came low and mournfully—"

Abruptly Tessa stopped singing. I faltered. Should I keep going?

"Let's not sing," she said.

"Oh, come on—" I urged her.

"You're off-key, Saige!" she finally blurted. "I can't stand it. It's like fingernails on a chalkboard."

I opened my mouth to answer, but nothing came out. I don't know much about singing. I mean, the last time we had music class was in second grade. But this wasn't a concert. It was just us having fun, the way we always used to.

Suddenly my chest felt as if it were full of cotton. I couldn't say a word—I was afraid I was going to cry. Tessa glanced over at me. She seemed worried, like she knew she'd hurt my feelings, but she didn't say anything either. We rode home in absolute silence.

Back home, I got into my pajamas and crawled into bed. Sam jumped up on the bed beside me. He isn't supposed to, but I let him sometimes, and right now I really needed him. I hugged his shaggy neck, and then the tears came.

Mimi was right when she'd said Tessa had grown a lot at music camp, but where did that leave me? Did Tessa think I was a baby now? *Was* I? I felt like one, huddled in bed with Sam licking hot tears off my cheeks.

One thing was for sure: I was never going to sing another note in front of Tessa. Maybe I *was* off-key. But did she have to say so?

Now I had a whole weekend to think about what had happened with Tessa—and what, if anything, I should do about it. Luckily the weather was great for ballooning, a perfect Albuquerque Box. That's when the lower winds blow north and the upper winds blow south. A pilot steers a balloon by changing how high he flies: blasting the burners to rise and go south or letting air out to sink down and go north.

The Box starts around dawn, so we were all up long before that on Saturday morning. We drove to the launch field and met the people Dad was taking up, a couple celebrating their anniversary.

I helped Dad get the balloon out of the pickup and spread the enormous envelope on the ground. The "envelope" is the balloon part, made out of super-strong nylon and polyester. The part that carries you is called the "basket."

After Dad filled the envelope with air using a big fan, we walked inside it, checking for holes and making sure the vents were sealed. If you need a dose of color—and wind—try walking inside a balloon envelope.

Then Dad blasted the propane burners, heating the air inside the balloon. The balloon rose, lifting the basket upright. Dad climbed in with his passengers. Mom released the tether, and we waited.

Sometimes we have to chase Dad's balloon in the truck, but with a perfect Box prevailing, Dad would be able to land where he started. We could just sit and watch.

I was still upset about what had happened with Tessa yesterday, but I didn't feel like talking about it with Mom. Luckily, there was no danger of that. She's *so* not a morning person. She should get a medal for having married a balloonist. She just clung to her coffee mug, listening to the news on the radio.

When Dad finally landed and his customers

left the launch field, Dad asked if I wanted to go up with him, just us two. I worried about that, because Dad is the bright-eyed early bird who catches the worm. He was bound to notice that something was bothering me.

But up in a balloon, you get taken over by a special kind of quiet. People don't talk much up there. As we drifted over the neighborhoods and *ranchitas*, that quiet got inside me. I stopped even thinking about Tessa. I just floated, looking down at houses and treetops, little cars and little people.

I did make a few decisions, though. I'd get going on that letter to the PTA, and I'd stop trying to get Tessa to help me. She clearly didn't want to, and I knew someone who did, someone who cared about art as much as I did.

Gabi and I walked to school together Monday morning, which was the new normal. She was quiet. Maybe she hadn't had the best weekend, either. "Do you still want to help me with that letter?" I asked, hoping to cheer us both up.

Gabi's pale face brightened. "Yes!" she said. "I thought you and Tessa had done it already."

I shook my head. I didn't want to get into that. "So, how do we start the letter?" I asked. "'Dear PTA'? That sounds weird."

"'To whom it may concern,'" Gabi said confidently. "That's how my mom starts letters like this. What do we say next?"

By the time we reached school, we had a few ideas. We sat at our table before class started and scribbled them all down.

I saw Tessa looking at me a little nervously. She probably wondered if I was mad at her about Friday night, but all I said to her was "Hi." As I'd hoped, there wasn't time to say much more.

At lunch, Gabi and I worked on the letter again. I wanted to say that it was stupid to not have art every year and that if the school system really cared about kids, they would change that.

"But we're not writing to the school board," Gabi said. "We're writing to the PTA. And anyway, the school system is probably doing the best it can. It's hard to get money, Saige. My mom says that art is being cut in schools all over the country."

"You're too nice," I grumped.

"Sorry," Gabi said, laughing.

A part of me still wanted to write something

angry, maybe because I was looking at Dylan and
Tessa making their stupid rubber-jaw faces. But what
Gabi said made sense. We scribbled out a final draft,
and I put it in my backpack to type up and print
at home.

After school I rode the bus to Mimi's, without
saying more than hi and bye to Tessa all day. I should
have felt good about that. It was just what I'd planned.
But I felt empty. Nothing felt right until I walked
through Mimi's door and she said, "Good!"

"Today I'll teach you how to ride in a parade,"
she announced over lemonade.

I was startled. "What do you mean?" I asked.
"I know how to ride."

"Parade riding is different," Mimi said.
"Picasso needs to be impressive, thrilling, slow, and
safe, all at the same time. Drink up, and I'll show you
what I mean."

Out in the corral, Mimi got on Picasso and
demonstrated. "This is a normal Western jog," she
said, signaling Picasso to trot slowly with his head
low. "He can keep this up for hours."

Then Mimi sat straighter and taller, deeper

in the saddle. She held the reins high. Her free hand hung straight down at her side.

Picasso seemed to get taller, too. He arched his neck, high and proud, and quickened his step. His trot became high-stepping, slow, and majestic. I could imagine a *conquistador* on his back, in glittering armor.

Mimi circled the ring and then brought Picasso to the fence. They were both breathing hard. "Your turn," Mimi said with a smile.

I felt a little nervous getting on *that* Picasso. *That* Picasso was royalty. But as I strapped on my helmet and walked over to him, he turned his head to look at me with his usual kind expression. I got on and asked him to jog, and Mimi coached me.

"Sit straighter," she called from the edge of the corral. "Sit deeper . . . lower your heels. Good. Now lift your rein hand higher."

Picasso kept jogging, low and slow. Only his ears changed, swiveling like Mimi's old rabbit-ears TV antenna, as if to say, *What are you up to, girl?*

"He's not getting it," Mimi said, holding up her hand for us to stop. "It's not your fault, Saige. He and I are such old partners that we have a private language. Let me think for a minute."

I let Picasso stand still, patting his sweaty

shoulder. He tossed his head, making the reins slap against his neck.

"That's it!" Mimi announced.

She jogged to the barn and came back with her fancy reins. They're heavy with silver ornaments and fasten to the bit with big decorated buckles—made by Luis, of course. Mimi put them on Picasso.

"Now jog him around the ring," she instructed. "Sit straight and deep, and lift your hand."

As we started to jog, the silver buckles clinked. Picasso's ears swiveled, listening.

I sank deeper in the saddle and tried to let my spine grow like a tree. I lifted my rein hand level to my chest. My free hand hung at my side, the way Mimi's had.

Suddenly it happened. Picasso seemed to grow taller. His head came up. His ears slanted proudly. The buckles made a bold *cling-cling-cling.* Picasso was doing his parade gait, and it felt amazing. What a powerful, incredible horse!

Parade riding was a lot harder than regular riding, though. I was panting when Mimi said, "Let him walk now."

"Wow!" I gasped, slowing Picasso down to a walk.

"Yeah," Mimi said, smiling. "You two *looked* like wow!"

"Why did changing the reins help?" I asked.

"I use those for parades, so they remind him of his parade gait," explained Mimi.

Picasso shook his head as she spoke, making the buckles ring. The sound reminded me of something, too. What was it? Just the tiniest jingle when she moved her head—

*Tessa!* Tessa's gorgeous bead earrings. I love those earrings, and they'd be perfect to wear to the fiesta. Picasso and I would both jingle. Would Tessa let me borrow them?

Until last Friday, I would have known the answer. I would have called or texted her the minute I got home. Now, I wasn't sure—and I was afraid to ask.

On Tuesday Gabi and I passed around the PTA letter in our classroom and at lunchtime for kids to sign. Gabi and I found out that *everybody* missed art. We asked kids to put a star beside their name if they were willing to help sell cookies and raffle tickets at the fiesta, and we got lots of stars.

Tessa and Dylan signed the letter, but without
stars. Dylan said they were too busy for bake sales.

By the end of the school day, we had forty-four
names. I couldn't believe it! A week ago, fund-raising
at the fiesta had seemed like a chore. But now that
more people were getting involved, it seemed like
fun. I couldn't wait to see how much money we would
raise!

I told Mimi all about the letter as we set up our
work in the studio that afternoon. "I had a hard time
getting going on it," I admitted, "but Gabi really
helped."

"You and I are alike that way," Mimi said.
"We both get more done when we have company."

We grinned across the studio at each other.
"You train horses alone, though," I said.

"No," Mimi said. "I always have the horse for
company."

Just then the gray kitten raced through the
studio, with Rembrandt in hot pursuit. His flying
paws bunched up the rug.

"Kids!" Mimi warned. "Calm down." She
bent over to straighten out the rug and then took
the opportunity to stretch, extending her finger-
tips toward her toes. She flexed one knee and then

the other. After a moment, Mimi stood back up and asked, "How's the painting coming? Will you finish it in time?"

The fiesta was about two and a half weeks away. I glanced down at my portrait of Picasso, which was looking a bit more like him every day. "It's almost ready," I said.

"Good! The difference between an artist and somebody who's artistic is that an artist *finishes* things. No pressure, of course!" said Mimi with a laugh.

Friday afternoon, Mrs. Applegate told us that our music teacher was out sick, so our class would have an unscheduled study break. Dylan and Gabi both headed to the computer lab at the back of the room, but Tessa asked for a library pass and then looked at me uncertainly. We used to love getting away to the library together.

"Want to come?" she asked.

"Sure!" I said, thrilled that she'd asked. Things had been weird between us ever since the singing incident.

We went to our favorite table, off in a corner

of the library where we could study but also talk. We did our English homework first, and things seemed so normal between us that I felt okay asking, "May I borrow your dangly earrings—those ones that jingle—to wear in the parade?"

"Of course!" she said, seeming happy that I had asked.

"Thanks," I said. "They'll match Picasso's fancy reins." I told her about Picasso's parade gait, Mimi's trick riding, and our paintings.

"Our singing group—" Tessa started to say.

"We're raffling tickets to ride up with Dad during one of the balloon ascensions," I said quickly. "He's making a ticket booth shaped like a hot-air balloon. It should be really cool, and we can use it again if we do another fiesta next year."

I was going on and on and on. I tried to stop, but my mouth just kept gabbing. "We should do this every year, don't you think? Because every year we're missing out on—"

"Saige!" Tessa interrupted, her cheeks flushing bright pink. "Do you realize that all you talk about is that fiesta?"

I could feel my mouth hanging open. Her comment was so unfair! I hadn't talked to Tessa about

47

*anything* for at least a week. "Well, all you talk about is music," I snapped.

Tessa looked shocked and hurt. "Music is my *life*," she said.

"Well, art is mine," I said, trying to hold my voice steady, "and this fiesta is going to help us get at least a little bit of art in school."

"But what about music?" Tessa asked, her voice trembling. "Next year we won't have music. You aren't trying to do anything about that!"

I hesitated. "But . . . but I would help *you*," I stammered, "if you were trying to get more music at school. You haven't helped me at all!"

Tessa snapped her dictionary shut. "I didn't help you because you don't need me," she said. "You have Gabi."

I was stunned. Was Tessa jealous of Gabi? How *could* she be when she spent all of her free time with Dylan? I opened my mouth to say that, but the librarian approached our table, raising her finger to her lips.

Tessa didn't say another word. She gathered her things, pushed back her chair, and stormed out of the library. I sat staring after her. That was *Tessa*, my best friend, walking out on me.

Tessa had been my friend since second grade. But we weren't best friends anymore, were we? Could we be best friends when we didn't like the same things or do the same things?

After school, I rode the bus to Mimi's, leaning my forehead against the window to hide my tears. I wasn't mad anymore, but my heart ached. Tessa and I had never fought like that before.

"Are you crying?" a first-grader behind me asked, sounding very sweet and concerned.

I shook my head, swallowing hard.

A siren shrieked behind us. The bus pulled to the side of the road, and an ambulance passed, going fast. As the bus pulled onto the road again, I sat up straighter. We were almost at Mimi's now, and I couldn't wait to pour out everything to her and ask for her advice.

When we got to my stop, the driver leaned forward, staring out his side window at Mimi's driveway. He said something as I got out, but I didn't catch it. I crossed in front of the bus and stopped at the edge of the road, confused.

The ambulance was in Mimi's yard, red lights

flashing, doors wide open. Carmen, Luis's wife, stood next to it, talking on a cell phone.

For a second I just stood there. I couldn't move. It felt as if all the air had been sucked out of my lungs. I couldn't call to Carmen. I couldn't even breathe.

My feet finally took off, and I sprinted up the driveway, but my brain still couldn't process what was going on. "What happened? Carmen, *what happened*?" I asked, almost screaming the words.

Carmen reached out and pulled me into a warm hug.

"Is Professor Marina Copeland available?" she spoke into the phone. "Yes, it's important. There's been an accident—her mother-in-law has fallen."

Carmen glanced down at me while waiting. "She's going to be okay, Saige," she said soothingly. "Mimi will be okay. She's—"

Back to the phone. "Hello? Yes, she fell in her studio. Luis found her. The ambulance is here now. . . . I'll tell her. Yes, Saige is right here. She just got off the bus." Carmen handed me the phone.

"Saige, I'll be there in half an hour!" Mom said before I could even say hello. I could tell that she was walking as she spoke, probably scattering university students out of her path. "Is your grand-mother conscious?"

"I . . . don't know," I said. "I haven't seen her."

"Tell her we'll be with her soon," Mom said firmly. "Find out which hospital they're taking her to, and wait with Carmen. I'll get ahold of Dad."

Luis came out of the house then, and I pressed the phone back into Carmen's hand and rushed to him. "How is she?" I asked breathlessly. "Can I see her now?"

Luis took my arms in his strong grip and looked straight into my eyes. He looked so serious that it scared me, but he spoke in a calm, steady voice. "She's probably broken some bones, Saige," he said. "She doesn't feel too good."

"What happened?" I asked.

"Something about the cat and dog—she tripped over one of them," said Luis. "You know how fast she's always moving. I think she's hurt her arm and her hip."

In the doorway behind him, men appeared carrying a stretcher—carrying Mimi. She looked small lying there, her hair messed up and her face yellow-white. Her right arm lay strapped across her stomach. Her breath came in short, quick gasps.

When she saw me, her eyes focused a little. "Good!" she whispered. "Luis and Carmen will . . . take care of you."

I rushed to Mimi's side, but I was afraid to touch her. "Oh, Mimi," was all I could say.

I heard Carmen asking the men which hospital

they were taking Mimi to, and then I remembered
Mom's instructions. "We'll be with you soon,"
I promised Mimi.

The medics loaded her into the back of the
ambulance. One climbed in beside her, one hopped
behind the wheel, and then they were gone.

I turned back toward the house, feeling numb.
Rembrandt slunk out, tail tucked up under his belly.
"He was beside her when I arrived," Luis said. "He
barked when I came in—asking for help, I think."

I crouched down beside Rembrandt. He crept
into my arms, shaking all over. "Poor boy," I said,
kissing his furry head.

I took Rembrandt inside and gave him his
supper, but he turned away from it miserably. I was
miserable, too. I couldn't stand to be in here with no
Mimi. I went back outside and waited with Luis and
Carmen. *Mom,* I thought. *Please hurry!*

At last her car pulled into the driveway. I ran
to the passenger door as Mom spoke to Luis and
Carmen through her open window. "Thank you both
so much!" she said. "I don't know what would have
happened if you hadn't been here."

As I buckled my seat belt, Mom reached over
to squeeze my hand. Then she turned the car around,

and we took off down the road, much faster than we usually drive.

When we reached the hospital, we found out that Mimi had been taken to the emergency room. Mom asked a nurse to tell Mimi we were there, and then we sat in the waiting room—and worried.

After what seemed like a very long time, Dad rushed into the waiting room, still wearing his pilot's uniform. He looked tired and anxious. "How is she?" he asked.

Mom started to fill him in, but just then a doctor appeared in the doorway and said, "Can I speak with the Copeland family?"

When we jumped up, she explained what was going on. Mimi had broken her femur, the bone in her thigh, just below the hip.

"That's good news," the doctor said. "A broken hip would have been much more serious. We'll need to put a pin in, and we've scheduled the operation for first thing tomorrow. She's also broken her wrist—not badly, but it will make recovery more difficult. We like to get people up as quickly as possible, but with a broken wrist, she may have trouble using a regular walker. We'll have to figure something out."

"Can we see her?" Dad asked.

"We're getting her settled in a room right now," said the doctor. "Someone will let you know when she's ready. But don't expect her to be too alert. We've given her medication to keep her comfortable."

Mom called Carmen to let her know what was happening, and then we all suddenly realized how hungry we were. We ate some lukewarm *fajitas* down in the cafeteria, and by the time we came back upstairs, they'd settled Mimi into a room.

When I saw her, the *fajita* turned into a cold lump in my stomach. Mimi's face was white, her hair still messy. She had a splint on her right arm, and a clear plastic tube fed some liquid into her left arm. She opened her eyes when we came in, but she didn't say anything, and her eyes quickly closed again.

We sat for a while, with Mom stroking Mimi's forehead and Dad squeezing the fingers of her good hand. When visiting hours ended, I leaned close to Mimi's face, hoping she would open her eyes and give me a special look, a word—anything. But Mimi's eyes stayed closed. I kissed her cheek, and we went back to the *ranchita*.

Luis and Carmen were waiting there with a steaming pot of hot chocolate. We sat around the kitchen table, and Mom and Dad updated Luis and

Carmen on Mimi's condition. Rembrandt sat beneath my chair, his body pressed up hard against my leg. I should have been mad at him, I guess, but I knew he felt terrible already. He hadn't meant to hurt Mimi, and neither had the kitten.

"Who's going to take care of Rembrandt—and the kitten?" I asked suddenly.

"He'll have to come home with us," Dad said, nodding toward Rembrandt, and I saw Mom grimace. Rembrandt and Sam may be brothers, but like some siblings, they don't get along.

"We'll check in on the kitten, honey," said Carmen, reaching over to squeeze my shoulder.

As we sipped our hot chocolate, we tried to figure out what chores needed doing on the *ranchita*. The chickens had gone into the coop at sunset. Their door needed to be locked each night so that skunks and coyotes didn't eat them—or their eggs.

"I'll feed the chickens in the morning, and check the horses," Luis said. "I do that sometimes when Mimi's away, so I know the routine."

The horses were on pasture and only needed their water tub filled. But Mimi checks on them twice a day, to make sure everyone's all right.

"May I go check the animals now?" I asked.

I wanted to be alone for a few minutes.

I found Mimi's flashlight, stepped outside, and went to check on the chickens. They were all lined up on their roost, crooning sleepily in the flashlight beam. I closed the door and locked it.

Then I went out to the horse corral. At first I didn't see any animals there. The horses graze in the evening, when the air is cool, and they have acres of pasture to scatter across. I checked the water tub, which was about half full. I turned on the hose and waited, looking up at the crescent moon in the velvet-dark New Mexico sky.

Mimi in the hospital—how could that be? Yesterday she was galloping on Picasso. Today she lay in that bed, looking broken.

A scuff and a gentle snort made me turn. Picasso was walking toward me. Maybe he'd heard the water gurgle. I slipped between the fence rails and went to greet him.

Picasso put his muzzle to my cheek and puffed his breath on me softly. Could he smell the hospital? Could he smell Mimi?

I leaned against Picasso's neck, breathing his rich horsey scent. "She's hurt, Picasso," I said. My voice came out all wobbly, and I didn't say anything more. I felt strange—clearheaded, but weak and shaky.

Mimi fell.

*Mimi* fell . . .

She'd seemed so unlike herself, lying there in that hospital bed. That wasn't the strong, full-of-life Mimi that I knew and loved.

But if Mimi wasn't Mimi, then I wasn't me. My whole world seemed turned upside down.

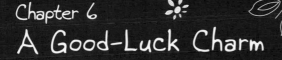
It was past eleven when we got home with Rembrandt. I went into the house first and let Sam out into the fenced backyard by himself. We don't usually do that, because Sam is a great jumper, but this late at night he wouldn't wander.

That was the theory, anyway, which lasted a whole thirty seconds—the time it took for Dad to lead Rembrandt up to the front door. Smelling his brother, Rembrandt woofed.

Sam let loose a huge peal of barks from the backyard. Dad hustled Rembrandt inside and into his and Mom's bedroom while I went out back to hush Sam.

He was nowhere to be seen but everywhere to be heard. Barks rang out from beside the house and then around front. I rushed to the front door and found him sniffing up and down the sidewalk. I called and he came racing in, only to bark at the bedroom door. Rembrandt barked back.

I dragged Sam to my room, and gradually things got quieter. Not quiet enough, though. Every time I started drifting off to sleep, one of the dogs woofed, and the other answered. Moans from Mom and yelling from Dad made no difference, especially when the Chihuahua next door started yipping, too.

In the morning, bleary-eyed and groggy, we went to the hospital.

Mimi was already being prepped for surgery, so we couldn't see her. We sat in a waiting room and looked at magazines for what seemed like forever, until the surgeon finally came out.

The operation had gone well, he said. He'd put in a pin to stabilize the bone. Mimi's broken leg might be slightly shorter than the other one, but that should be the only lasting effect.

We sat with Mimi in the recovery room. She slept, looking pale in the white bed, with her graying hair spread across the pillow. We all kept yawning while we waited for her to wake up. Finally Mimi opened her eyes wide. I could see it took a huge effort.

When she focused her eyes on our own tired faces, Mimi's face suddenly looked stern. Her lips moved, but I couldn't hear what she said. She pointed to the cup on her bedside table. Mom brought it to her and bent the straw so that she could drink.

After a long sip of water, Mimi whispered hoarsely, "Go home. Take a nap!"

Mom and I looked at each other and grinned. Mimi bossing us around—that was a good sign!

Dad asked, "How do you feel, Ma?"

# A Good-Luck Charm

"Stupid," Mimi said with a frown. "What a stupid, stupid thing to do!"

She was talking about her accident. But Mimi never puts herself down, or anyone else, either. When I heard how angry she was with herself, I felt like crying. Maybe she did, too.

Mom asked more questions, and Mimi told us that she didn't feel too bad, just tired. Very tired. She closed her eyes again. Clearly she didn't want to talk, or she couldn't.

We went to the cafeteria for an early lunch, but I couldn't eat. My stomach was in knots. When we came back, Luis and Carmen were visiting. Mimi looked livelier, but no happier. "*Old ladies* break their hips," she was telling Carmen.

Carmen said, "You didn't break your hip, Mimi. You broke your leg. Even a kid can do that."

"That was all I could think, lying there," Mimi said. "You've broken your hip. You just turned into an old lady."

"Nonsense, Ma," Dad said in the blustery voice he uses when he thinks someone is overreacting. "You'll bounce right back from this!"

Mimi turned her head to focus on Dad, and she looked annoyed—even mad. She shot something back at him, but I didn't hear what she said, because Luis tapped my arm. "It's getting crowded in here," he whispered, jerking his thumb toward the hall.

"Mimi will be more herself tomorrow," he said when we were outside the room. "But she's scared, Saige. This takes away her two most important things—riding and painting."

"But she'll get better," I said. "People get better from broken legs."

For a long, scary moment, Luis didn't answer. He looked over my head, back into Mimi's room. "Mimi's going to miss the ranch," he said. "It's hard for someone like Mimi to recover in a place like this."

I glanced around. I hadn't noticed before, because I'd been so worried, but the hospital was like our school hallway times ten. Everything was white or pale yellow—a haze of blandness that stretched on as far as the eye could see.

"Do you think . . .?" I began. "Could I bring in some of Mimi's things tomorrow?"

"Good idea!" Luis said. "Let's ask the nurse. It'll make Mimi feel better."

I peeked back into the room. Mimi looked a little more normal now. Arguing with Dad had brought a touch of color to her cheeks.

## A Good-Luck Charm

That was it—color! There was nothing bright or rich or interesting to look at here, nothing to think about. It was a hospital. I couldn't change that. But I could change *something*.

Sunday morning Luis did the chores at Mimi's, and we slept in—or tried to. It wasn't really possible with the dog situation.

In the afternoon we stopped at the *ranchita* before we went to the hospital. When we walked into Mimi's house, no one said "Good!" No Rembrandt barked. The kitten sat quite still on a kitchen stool, her tail wrapped around her paws. Her food and water bowls looked full. I said a silent *thank you* to Carmen for that.

While Dad and Mom looked for some insurance papers in Mimi's office, I fed and watered the chickens, collected the eggs, and looked the horses over thoroughly, the way Mimi would have. They were fine, and it felt so good to hug Picasso. Some horses wiggle when you put your arms around their necks, but he just stood there, solid and comforting.

While I was leaning on him, Luis appeared. "Got an idea," he said.

He had a pair of steel scissors with him, and he reached up under Picasso's mane and snipped off a lock of hair. I sucked in my breath.

Luis smiled down at me. "I know," he said. "But she's not here, is she? And I think she'll like what I'm going to do with this. Want to watch?"

He took the chunk of hair to the kitchen and laid out some small metal objects on the table: a jewelry clasp, some silver beads, and a pair of needle-nose pliers. Luis began straightening the horse hairs, combing and pulling them between his fingers until they were all in line. He crimped a piece of silver that looked like a row of staples onto the end with the pliers. "Can you hold this for me, Saige?" he asked.

Luis's fingers, which looked too big and muscular for such delicate work, started braiding. It was a complicated four-strand braid, with only a few hairs in each strand. Picasso's silver-white mane hair kept disappearing, and Luis occasionally paused and squeezed his eyes shut, without ever letting go of the hairs between his fingers. I kept a tight grip on the other end of the hairs as he braided.

When the braid was complete, Luis pinched another set of silver staples onto the end and attached a jewelry clasp. Suddenly it was obvious to me what he had been making.

"A bracelet!" I exclaimed.

"Yes. A charm to bring Mimi back to us," Luis said, handing me the bracelet. "Give it to her today, and tell her that I'll stop by tomorrow morning."

That reminded me of my task. I wanted to gather some colorful things for Mimi, and I had a list: The deep-red *serape* that was draped over the chair. A painting of the horses. A photo of Rembrandt standing on the porch with his mouth wide open, panting.

I wanted to bring some art supplies, too. If Mimi could still move her fingers, she could doodle, and that might remind her of who she was, the way the fancy reins had reminded Picasso.

I grabbed a sketchpad. Then I poked through the cups of drawing instruments until I found the perfect thing—a felt-tipped brush-pen, just like mine. It's easy to use and makes a deep black line with only the slightest pressure.

When Mom and I got to the hospital, Mimi was sitting in a wheelchair—not the bed—and watching television. She turned her head sharply toward the door when I knocked and said, "Good!"

A huge grin spread over my face. I dumped

things onto her chair and bent to kiss her. "You look better," I said with relief.

"I feel better," Mimi agreed. "I talked with the surgeon today, and he's confident that he can get me up walking again. I don't know about *riding* . . ."

A shadow of worry crossed Mimi's face. I jumped in before she could think about that for a moment longer. "Luis sent you this," I said brightly, holding out the bracelet.

Mimi reached for it with her left hand, cupped the bracelet, and turned it awkwardly toward her to get a closer look. "Oh! Is it—"

"Picasso's mane. But don't worry," I reassured her. "You can't see where Luis cut it off at all."

"Glad to hear it!" said Mimi in a sort-of-teasing, sort-of-stern voice. "Picasso needs to look good for the parade."

*The parade.* I hadn't been thinking about that, or the fiesta. How could Picasso and I possibly lead the parade without Mimi there? And would there even *be* a fiesta without Mimi's trick riding? It was the main act! My hopes for the after-school arts program *whooshed* out of me like air from a balloon.

To distract myself from those depressing thoughts, I turned to the bag of things I had brought from the ranch. While Mom fastened the bracelet onto Mimi's left wrist, I opened the red *serape* and draped it over the chair. I took down the hospital's generic seagulls-and-surf picture and hung Mimi's horse painting. I put Rembrandt's photo on Mimi's bedside table, and in front of it, I put the sketchpad and the felt-tipped pen.

I looked up to see Mimi watching me. Her eyes sparkled with tears.

"Life's blood," she said in a choked voice. "You're my life's blood, Saige. Thank you."

I swallowed the lump in my throat and reached out to hold Mimi's outstretched hand.

I saw tears in Mom's eyes, too. She quickly wiped them away and smiled at Mimi. "Let me brush and put up your hair," Mom said. "You'll feel more like yourself."

As Mom brushed Mimi's hair, Mimi told us more about her expected recovery. The news wasn't all good. Because Mimi had broken both an arm and a leg, she said, her doctor thought her recovery would be complicated, especially without anyone at home to help.

"I'll stay with you," I said quickly. Mom started to say something, too.

Mimi cut her off. "Out of the question," she said. "I'll need help twenty-four hours a day for a while, and that's too much to ask of anyone. I'm just hoping you and Luis can manage the animals for a month or six weeks while I go to the rehab center and let the professionals get me going."

I tried to hide my disappointment. I wouldn't get to live with Mimi after all.

"Anyway, Saige," she told me, squeezing my hand again, "you'll have plenty to do keeping the fiesta on track."

At that, my anxiety about the fiesta came rushing back. I wasn't even sure I wanted to be a part of it anymore—not without Mimi by my side.

Back at home that night, I thought again about Mimi's words. How was *I* supposed to keep the fiesta on track?

I took a deep breath, sat down at my desk, and made a list: Get Picasso in shape for the parade. Remind my classmates about the bake sale. Finish my painting. How could I get these things done? And would any of it matter if we didn't have a main act— something to replace Mimi's trick riding?

The dogs weren't helping. They needed constant attention because they quarreled about *everything*: Food. Toys. Who went through the door first. Who got walked first. Every little thing that used to be easy was now complicated.

I crawled into bed and pulled the covers over my head. It was too much!

The next morning, Sam insulted Rembrandt, or Rembrandt insulted Sam, and they wouldn't stop barking. I had to walk them separately, and by the time that was done, I was running too late to walk to school with Gabi. Mom dropped me off, and I slid into my chair at our table.

"How's your grandmother?" Gabi whispered.

"Better," I whispered back.

"What happened? Did she fall off a horse?"

"She's going to get so tired of that question," I said. "No, she tripped over Rembrandt." *She might like saying **that**,* I thought. I mean, how many artists can say, "I broke my leg tripping over Rembrandt"? I hoped we'd be joking about that soon.

But Gabi wasn't laughing. She was looking at me wide-eyed, and so was Dylan. Even Tessa was all ears, as if our argument last week had never happened. I was grateful for that.

"Mimi broke her leg just below the hip," I explained, "and she broke her wrist, too—her right wrist."

Tessa looked aghast. "Her painting hand?" she asked.

"Yes," I said solemnly.

Without warning, tears welled up in my eyes and ran over. I sat there helplessly watching them drip onto the table, trying not to sob.

For a long, awkward moment, I couldn't look up at my friends, and no one seemed to know what to do. Then Tessa—good old Tessa—handed me a tissue and put her face close to mine.

"She'll be fine, you know," she said. "She's

*Mimi."* Tessa reached for my hand and gave it a squeeze.

I nodded, sniffled, and took a deep, ragged breath. I didn't know if Tessa was right about Mimi, but I did know now that she was still my friend, and that helped. It helped a lot.

Tuesday morning before breakfast, I was trying to put on Rembrandt's leash, but he wasn't cooperating. On the other side of the table, Mom held Sam, who barked and strained to break free. He thought Rembrandt was hurting me—or maybe just getting too much of my attention.

Just then both dogs looked toward the front door and began barking identical loud *woof*s.

"Did you hear something?" Mom shouted over the uproar.

The doorbell *ding-dong*ed, and Rembrandt dragged me to the door. I opened it a crack, twisting the leash around my hand.

Gabi stood on the front step, and she didn't seem at all freaked out by the barking and yelling going on inside the house. "I came to help you with the dogs," she said over the din. "I saw you trying to walk them together last night."

As I pulled Rembrandt away from the door, Gabi slipped inside and stood still, letting him sniff her closed fist the way she'd done with Sam. He stopped barking to greet her.

"Mom, this is Gabi," I said. "From down the street. She wants to help with the dogs."

Mom nodded but said nothing—Sam was still barking too loudly. But I noticed that Rembrandt was paying close attention to Gabi, especially to her jeans pocket.

"Give me the leash," Gabi said. "And can you lock Sam away somewhere?"

I led Sam into my bedroom and struggled to close the door behind me. As I walked back toward the kitchen, I heard a *click*, like an empty soda can when you press it with your thumb.

Gabi gave Rembrandt a treat from her pocket, and then she made the clicking sound again. It came from a little plastic box in her hand. She gave Rembrandt another treat. *Click*, treat. *Click*, treat.

From behind me, Sam barked wildly and scrabbled on my door. Rembrandt turned toward the door and gave a bossy woof, and then he turned back to Gabi.

*Click*, treat.

He gobbled it and then sat and looked straight at Gabi's face, ignoring Sam. *Click*, treat.

After a few repeats, Gabi led Rembrandt down the hall toward my room. The sound of his toenails on the floor sent Sam into a frenzy again. I was sure Rembrandt would bark back, but Gabi managed to keep his attention with clicks and treats. They passed right by my door, and all Rembrandt did was make a disapproving expression with his ears.

"I'll take him outside now," Gabi said. "You bring Sam. Put some of these treats in your pocket, and any time he looks at you instead of us, say 'Good!' and give him one. Okay?" She handed me some treats and then led Rembrandt out the front door.

I looked at Mom. Was she okay with Gabi walking in and taking charge of the dogs?

"That girl is a miracle worker!" Mom said, grinning broadly.

Yep, she was okay with it. I stuffed the handful of treats into my pocket and opened the door of my room. Sam charged out, looking for his bossy brother.

"Sammy!" I said.

He barely glanced at me, but that was probably the best he could do right now. "Good boy!" I said, dropping a treat on the floor.

Sam made a U-turn and snarfed it. "Sit," I said.
"Good boy." I gave him another treat, put his leash on,
and led him outside.

Gabi had Rembrandt halfway down the
street, walking on a loose leash. Sam barked at him.
Rembrandt started to answer and then checked in
with Gabi. *Click,* treat.

"Sammy," I said, "do you want a treat?"

That was probably cheating. "Treat" is a word
Sam knows well. He looked up at me eagerly, and
I gave him another treat.

Then I turned and walked Sam the opposite
way down the street. He wanted to look over his
shoulder at Rembrandt, but I called his name, and he
looked at me instead. By the time we got to the far
end of the street, he was able to do his business and
read all the "messages" left by other dogs on the
telephone pole.

Once Gabi had Rembrandt back inside, I went
in with Sam. Rembrandt was already in Mom and
Dad's room. Mom handed me one of Sam's rubber
toys, stuffed with peanut butter, and I put him in my
room. Blissful silence settled upon the house.

"Magical!" Mom breathed.

I bolted my breakfast while Gabi explained what she'd been doing. "Every time Rembrandt looked at me instead of Sam," she said, "I gave him a treat. He learned really quickly."

"But what was that noise?" I asked.

"A clicker," said Gabi, holding up a small blue plastic box. "I clicked and gave him a treat, clicked and gave him a treat, until he knew that's what the click meant—a treat coming. Then I clicked when he was doing what I wanted, like looking at me instead of Sam. He started to think, *If I look at her, I can make her click and give me a treat.* After a while I stretched out the time, so he had to look longer and longer before he got clicked."

"I want to know a lot more about this," Mom said. "But right now, *thank you,* Gabi. You've restored peace to this neighborhood!"

The bus streaked by the window. I gulped my orange juice. "Let's go," I said to Gabi as I grabbed my backpack.

As we hurried toward school, I asked Gabi more about clicker training. "So, does this work on horses, too?" I asked.

"Sure," said Gabi. "We taught my aunt's horse to do tricks using a clicker."

I turned to face Gabi, walking backward to keep pace with her. "What kind of tricks?" I asked.

"Answering questions by nodding yes or no," Gabi said matter-of-factly. "Counting. Laughing."

"*Laughing?* Really?" I had seen Gabi do some pretty amazing things with her clicker, but this I didn't believe.

"No, you know," Gabi said, "like this." She curled her upper lip, showing her teeth. Then I understood. Horses do that when they smell something strange. It's what people call a "horse laugh." It isn't really laughing, but it looks funny. And it was giving me an idea.

Mimi had asked me to keep the fiesta on track. I didn't know how to do that all by myself, but with my new friend Gabi—who was so good at training animals—by my side, maybe the show *could* go on. I felt something swell in my chest, and then I could barely get the words out fast enough.

"Could you teach Picasso some tricks?" I asked Gabi. "Because Mimi can't do her act for the fiesta. Picasso is *so* smart. Maybe we can teach him some new tricks! Maybe we can do our *own* show with him."

At first Gabi was speechless. Then I saw the

spark of excitement in her eyes, too. "Sure," she said. "I mean, I don't know. We don't have a ton of time, and my aunt did most of the training, but . . . *yes*, we can try!"

That was good enough for me. I gave Gabi a quick hug. And then the school bell rang and we started sprinting, Gabi and I, laughing and talking as we ran.

After school, I visited Mimi at the rehab center, where she had been moved that morning. It was in the same complex as the hospital, but as I walked through the front door, I immediately liked it better. Instead of sick people in beds, I saw lots of people getting around on walkers and crutches. And there was some beautiful art on the walls, including oils and watercolors.

Mimi was in a wheelchair in her room and looked exhausted. Mom said that she'd been up walking with physical therapists twice already, and I could tell that it had hurt.

But when I asked Mimi how she felt about Gabi and me teaching Picasso tricks, her face lit up. "I've been worried about the fiesta," she admitted. "This is perfect! Don't teach him counting, though. I've spent a lifetime teaching him not to paw."

I was disappointed at first, but I knew what Mimi meant. A horse that paws the ground when you want it to stand still can be very annoying. Luckily Gabi and I had a lot of other ideas.

The next morning, Gabi and I talked about the fiesta while we walked the dogs, with clickers and Sam's favorite treats in our pockets. Then we raced to school together. It was fun having a friend who lived almost next door. Getting together with Tessa meant a bike ride or finding somebody to drive us, but meeting Gabi was so easy.

We dropped into our seats at the table, still laughing and talking about Picasso. But while Gabi shared with me yet another idea for the act, I saw Tessa's expression over Gabi's shoulder. She was watching us out of the corner of her eye, as if she was interested in what we were saying but didn't feel like she was a part of it.

I could sure understand that—how left out you feel when two people are talking about something you don't know much about. I kind of wanted to say, *Get over it!* But another part of me wished Tessa *was* a part of the fiesta, that we could all plan for it and have fun with it together.

Then, as Tessa and Dylan started to make their cathedral-mouth faces, I had an idea. "Hey!" I said, leaning around Gabi to tap Tessa's shoulder. "You guys should sing at the fiesta! I mean, next year we won't have music at school, right? But if we have music at the fiesta, it would help make the point that art *and* music are important."

Tessa looked pleased. "Do you think we could?" she asked hesitantly. "Our singing group has been practicing a lot. I'd *love* to do something."

"Mimi's friend Celeste is in charge of the show," I said. "Do you want me to ask her? I have to talk to her about Picasso anyway."

Tessa and Dylan looked at each other again, and I could see the excitement spread across their faces. "Sure," Dylan said slowly. "Ask her." And for a moment everything felt different at our table—friendlier, happier.

That afternoon Gabi rode the bus with me out to the ranch for the first time ever. Carmen was there to keep an eye on us, and she'd brought a plate of warm, sweet *biscochitos*. They're a kind of sugar cookie, the state cookie of New Mexico. Some people save *biscochitos* for Christmas, but Carmen makes them year-round. It's only partly why I love her.

While we ate, we sliced some carrots into coin shapes. Then we headed to the stable, where I introduced Gabi to all the horses. After that, we brought Picasso to his stall.

Gabi was good with Picasso, just as she was with the dogs. She talked to him gently and patted him in his favorite places. I could tell she had been around horses before.

After a few minutes of getting to know Picasso, Gabi got down to business.

"Okay, let's see if this works," she said. She touched Picasso lightly at the base of his neck with one finger. "I'm pretending to be a fly." Sure enough, Picasso dipped his nose toward his chest to brush the "fly" off. *Click.* Carrot.

Picasso munched his carrot coin thoughtfully, looking Gabi over. He seemed to find her an odd girl, but interesting.

Gabi touched his chest again. Dip, *click*, carrot. This time it looked like a nod, like a yes.

Touch, nod, *click*, carrot. Touch, nod, *click*, carrot. After a few repeats, Picasso dipped his nose when Gabi was still reaching, before she even touched him. He got a whole handful of carrot slices for that.

"Good boy," I said proudly, patting his neck.

"Wow, it worked!" Gabi said. "I wasn't sure. Let's let him rest for a few minutes, and then maybe we can teach him to say no."

There was plenty for us to do while we gave Picasso a short break. We collected eggs and fed Mimi's chickens. We took the eggs into the house, washed them, and put them in egg boxes in the refrigerator. Then we went back out to see Picasso.

Gabi rehearsed him on nodding yes a couple of times. Then she reached her hand out to tickle the hair on Picasso's ear. Picasso shook his head, as if to say no. *Click*, carrot.

Gabi repeated that several times until Picasso had it down, and then she went back and forth a few times between having him nod yes and shake his head for no.

"We can't tickle him in the performance, though," I said. "Right?"

81

"No, we'll fade the signals," Gabi said.

When she saw the look of confusion on my face, she explained. "Already he nods when I reach toward his neck," she said. "Soon he'll do it when I just point my finger. And *you'll* be staring at his head, so that's where people will look. That's how magic shows work. If you look where you want the audience to look, they follow your eyes. You can give the hand cues right in front of them and they'll never notice."

The person I was staring at right now was Gabi. "How do you *know* all this?" I asked.

"I like doing tricks," Gabi said. "I told you—I want to train animals and maybe even have my own show someday."

"Well, you're definitely the star of this show!" I declared. "You and Picasso."

Gabi flushed, looking pleased. "Thanks," she said. "But what will we call the show? We need a name."

I looked at Picasso, who gave me a wise look back. "I know," I said. "We can call it the Professor Picasso Show!"

"That's perfect!" said Gabi. "And we'll be his Lovely Assistants."

"With lovely costumes," I added, already

imagining what I would wear.

"Picasso needs a costume, too," Gabi said thoughtfully. "What could we use?"

In the tack room, we found an old cotton ear net. It looked like a little cap, with two cloth ears and a triangle shape that hung over the horse's forehead, with crocheted fringe.

"Mimi uses this on Frida sometimes," I told Gabi. "The flies really bother her."

"It can be Picasso's Thinking Cap," Gabi said. "Though it's not very showy."

She was right. The ear net had been purple once, but now it was faded to lilac gray. "Fabric dye?" I suggested. "We could get it at the grocery store."

"Yes!" said Gabi. "And we could paint some glittery designs on the ears."

We spent the rest of the afternoon at Mimi's kitchen table, planning our costumes and sketching designs for Picasso's Thinking Cap. For a few moments, I actually forgot about Mimi's accident. With a drawing pencil in my hand and a good friend by my side, all seemed right with the world.

Thursday afternoon found Gabi and me back

at Mimi's horse stable, teaching Picasso how to say "duh."

Gabi did that by tickling Picasso's upper lip. He responded by curling it up in a huge, jeering horse laugh. I was laughing, too—so hard that I could barely stand up.

"What's so funny?" a voice asked from behind us. It was Luis. I showed him Picasso's new trick, and a broad smile spread across his face.

"What a genius!" said Luis, stroking Picasso's neck. "How's the parade gait going?"

*The parade gait.* My stomach sank. We'd been working so hard on the Professor Picasso Show that I'd hardly thought about the parade. Every once in a while, I'd remembered that I needed to practice, but there was never time. And now the art fiesta was only nine days away!

Luis gave me a sympathetic look. "Why don't you practice now, while I can watch you?" he suggested.

Luis helped me saddle up Picasso, but today, Picasso seemed to have no idea what I wanted him to do. Even his fancy silver reins didn't help us with the parade gait. I sat straight, I sat deep, I let my hand hang at my side—I even shook the reins gently so that they rang against the bit.

It was no use. Picasso's slender gray ears swiveled, but he just kept sedately jogging.

"Don't worry," Luis said. "When he gets to the head of the parade line and sees the crowd, he'll remember."

"Yes!" Gabi said. "That will be his cue."

I hoped Luis was right about Picasso. But what if he *wasn't*?

Friday afternoon, Gabi and I practiced the yes, no, and "duh" commands again with Picasso. He needed a little extra work with "duh," but Gabi was patient with him, and he got it down.

"He's so smart!" she said. "Most horses would take longer to learn these tricks. I wonder what else we can teach him."

I wondered, too, but not for long. By the time Gabi's mom dropped her off at the *ranchita* again on Saturday morning, Gabi had that excited look on her face that I'd come to know well. "I just talked with my aunt this morning, and she had a brilliant idea," Gabi said. "We should teach Picasso to paint!"

Brilliant, yes. Easy? No.

"We need an easel," Gabi told me.

I knew right where to find one of those. "Stay here," I said to Gabi. Then I ran into the house and down the hall toward the studio.

When I stepped into Mimi's studio, my stomach clenched. Our empty lemonade glasses were still there on the table. Everything was just as it had been the last time Mimi and I had painted together. I looked at the floor, half-expecting to see a chalk outline where Mimi had fallen. Nothing, of course—just hard tiles.

As I reached to take Mimi's painting off her easel, my hands froze. I couldn't do it. I didn't want to change a *thing* in that special place until Mimi was able to walk back into it with me.

Instead of taking the easel, I found a big sketchpad in the pile of art supplies behind the studio sofa. I took one last look at the empty studio and then forced myself to turn and hurry down the hall.

When I got back outside, I saw that Luis had joined Gabi and Picasso in the corral. He helped us fasten the sketchpad to the fence. Then Gabi set up a card table in front of it and put out an old brush for painting window sashes.

Picasso's eyes brightened when he saw the

setup. *Some new game?* he must have wondered. He pushed the brush around with his nose and then picked it up by the bristle end. It was sort of what we wanted, so Gabi clicked.

Picasso did it again, and again. But he wouldn't touch the brush handle—only the bristles.

"Okay, I taught him the wrong thing," Gabi said. "We have to stop clicking him for that, even though he's trying."

That was difficult for all of us. Picasso bit the brush. He flapped it around by the bristles, harder and harder. "Should we stop?" I asked.

"Wait," said Gabi.

That was Gabi's solution to every training problem. It seemed easy for her, but Picasso and I were getting frustrated.

*Click!*

"What was that for?" I asked Gabi.

"He touched the handle with his lip," she said. "Watch him."

Picasso's silver-white whiskers hovered near the bristle end of the brush. I saw his ears swivel. Then his mouth opened, and he very deliberately bit the handle.

*Click!*

"Yay, Picasso!" said Gabi, feeding him a huge handful of carrots. She put the brush back on the table, and Picasso seized it with his mouth.

"Picasso, you're a *genius*," I said. "You too, Gabi. This is going to work!"

Once Picasso would hold the brush, Gabi gave him the cue to nod. That swished the brush up and down the paper, which promptly wrinkled and tore.

By now, Gabi and I were getting pretty good at problem solving. A clamp at the bottom of the sketch-pad was the answer.

Next, it was time for paint. I brought out the finger paints Mimi had gotten for me when I was little. They're super-duper child-safe, made with vegetable dyes. We dipped the brush in the blue paint and laid it on the table.

Picasso flared his nostrils and followed the paint smell to the bristle end of the brush, getting a huge blue smudge on his nose.

We washed him off and had him practice grabbing the right end of the brush a few more times, loaded the brush with paint again, and waited.

Confidently, Picasso seized the handle. He lifted the brush and swept it across the canvas, making a bold blue streak.

*Click!* Gabi reached for the brush as Picasso dropped it, handed him a carrot, and dipped another brush—in yellow paint. This time Picasso made a wispy zigzag. I offered him an orange-loaded brush, and he painted with that as well.

When I took the brush away, Picasso lifted his muzzle and sniffed his painting thoughtfully. He twitched his lip across the blue streak, making a smudge on it and giving himself a blue mustache again.

Gabi collapsed, giggling. Picasso looked at us and lifted his blue lip in a laugh, which sent me into hysterics, too. When I could catch my breath, I washed off Picasso's muzzle and then carefully tore his painting off the sketchpad.

"How did he do?" asked Luis from beyond the fence.

I showed him the painting. "It's a Picasso original," I said proudly. "A true masterpiece."

I didn't plan to tell Mimi about Picasso's painting just yet. I was hoping more than anything that she'd somehow be able to come to the fiesta, and I wanted to surprise her there with Picasso's painting trick. But Mimi's recovery seemed to be moving slowly. She had been quiet all week.

"Just tired," she said Sunday, when I asked how she felt. "It's a lot of therapy." The corners of her mouth curved down. She looked sad and lined, and she was losing her tan.

"How's therapy going?" I asked, and then, "Will you be able to make it to the fiesta?" I hoped that talking about the fiesta would perk her up.

Mimi didn't answer. I took that for a no, and my stomach sank. Gabi and I had worked so hard on the Professor Picasso Show, but it hardly seemed worth doing if Mimi couldn't come.

I wanted to plead with Mimi, *Try! Try harder!* But I could tell by her face that she didn't want to talk, so we sat in silence. I wished Dad hadn't left the room. He'd gone to straighten something out about Mimi's insurance, and now the minutes passed like hours.

I tried again. "Well, how do they say you're doing?" I asked brightly.

Mimi laughed, sounding a little bitter. "Oh, they *say* I'm a marvel!" she said. "For a woman my age. But maybe they're just humoring me. I mean, I used to train horses. I ran a ranch. I painted professionally. What if these therapists are just hoping to help me drive a car again or go shopping?"

Mimi's dark mood scared me. What should I say? Why couldn't Dad hurry back?

But he wasn't here. I was. So I took a deep breath and tried my best. "It isn't up to them, Mimi. Right? It's up to you," I said, trying to sound more certain than I felt. "I mean, you could try drawing with your left hand. Think about those paralyzed people who paint holding the brush in their teeth or between their toes . . ."

Mimi looked up at me with a sad smile. "Thank you, dear," she said and patted my hand. I felt like I'd been dismissed, as if I were a small, well-meaning child who didn't understand big, grown-up problems. But Mimi had never treated me that way, even when I *was* a small child. I felt suddenly as if we were very far apart.

We fell into a painful silence again until Mimi asked, "How's your painting coming?"

*My painting?* Mimi meant the painting for the

auction. "I . . . haven't touched it," I confessed. I just hadn't felt like painting without Mimi there. And I *had* been pretty busy.

"I'm sorry to hear that," Mimi said. "Clearly I won't be finishing anything for the sale, either, so I want you to go through the stack of canvases behind the big chest and pick out something small but nice. One of the saddle still lifes, maybe."

"Okay," I answered, only half-listening. I knew Mimi wanted me to finish my own painting. But how could I? How could I get excited about painting when Mimi wouldn't be holding a paintbrush beside me?

Luckily Dad came back just then. He chatted with Mimi for a few minutes, but she hardly answered. Finally Dad looked at his watch. "Sorry, Ma," he said, "but Saige and I have a lot to do this weekend to prep for the fiesta. We'll have to cut it short today."

I bent to give Mimi a kiss. As I straightened back up, I noticed the brush-pen and pad of paper on Mimi's bedside table, poking out from under a book and Mimi's mail. I neatened things up on the table, making sure the pen and pad were on top.

As Dad and I drove home, I replayed my conversation with Mimi in my mind. I winced, remembering the disappointment I'd heard in her voice when she'd asked about my painting. She was right. I *had* to finish it for the auction.

I asked Dad to drop me off at the *ranchita* on the way home. I checked in with Luis and Carmen, to let them know I was there, and then I fed the chickens, collected eggs, and filled the horses' water tub. Finally, I walked into the studio, feeling nervous but determined.

Everything was just as we'd left it, of course: the pink horses on Mimi's easel and the portrait of Picasso on mine. The paint on my palette had dried. I peeled back the surface, and there was nice, squishy paint underneath. I picked up a brush.

To do what? I saw what the painting needed, but I didn't want to touch it. I felt flat inside. There's a space I go to when I'm painting, a timeless zone. I couldn't find it now. It wasn't like the door to that space was locked—it was like there was no door at all.

I looked over at Mimi's empty stool. *We both get more done when we have company,* she had said. She was right.

After ten discouraging minutes, I carefully cleaned my paintbrush and put it away. A big ball of sadness and anxiety was spinning in my stomach. The fiesta was less than a week away. I had to

finish my painting in the next couple of days so that
the paint would have time to dry. But I was afraid that
if I painted when I was feeling this way, I'd only spoil
something I'd put a lot of work into. Maybe I could try
again tomorrow.

I went out to see Picasso. I desperately needed
to ride him—to practice the parade gait. What if he
wouldn't do it for me on parade day? But I knew I
shouldn't get on a horse, even Picasso, feeling this
way. A rider needs to be calm and thoughtful, and
that was so not me right now. I stood there looking
at him and biting my nails, which I hadn't done since
the beginning of third grade.

Monday morning Tessa noticed my ragged
nails. Even though we aren't as close as we used to
be, nobody knows me better than Tessa. She sat down
beside me at lunch.

"How's Mimi?" she asked, looking at my
fingernails.

I hid them in my palms. "Better," I said, not
wanting to tell Tessa the truth about Mimi's mood.
"But I just can't make myself finish my painting.
I promised Mimi I'd have something to put in the

silent auction, but I *can't!*"

"Why not?" Tessa asked. Her voice was so sympathetic, I found myself telling her everything.

"I miss Mimi so much," I said. "We've always painted together. My painting brain just won't turn on when I'm in her studio alone."

"So, bring the painting home," Tessa suggested.

I mulled that over for a moment. I would rather work in Mimi's studio, but if I worked on the painting at home, at least I wouldn't be alone.

Then another idea occurred to me. "Would you . . . come out and paint with me tomorrow afternoon?" I asked Tessa hesitantly. "The way you used to?" Gabi couldn't come to the ranch tomorrow because she had to babysit, and I knew Tessa was free—she didn't have music lessons on Tuesday. It was the only day that might work.

For a moment Tessa looked past me, mulling it over. I waited through the silence for her response. I guess Gabi had taught me a thing or two about patience.

Tessa finally sighed and smiled. "Okay," she said. "I should be practicing, but I know this is important to you."

I almost couldn't believe it. Tessa had been so

fierce about protecting her practice time for the last month, it had started to seem like it was sacred. If Tessa would do this for me, then we were still friends. Good friends—no matter what.

Slowly, a little shyly, I squinched my face into a cat smile. Tessa cat-smiled back, and I felt better than I had in days.

The next afternoon, Tessa and I rode the bus to Mimi's house. I still wasn't sure this would work. Things with Tessa hadn't been easy lately. But having her in the studio seemed to loosen me up.

Tessa sat at the drawing table, doodling, while I peeled the skin off my dried-up oils and stared at my painting. *Deepen the background now,* those shadows were telling me. *Add some purple. And possibly some blue in the top corner?*

I started to paint, listening to the artist's voice in my head. Dimly, as if far away, I heard gentle notes from Mimi's guitar. For a moment, I thought Mimi was in the studio beside me. I whirled around to find Tessa sitting on the studio couch, picking out a slow tune on Mimi's guitar.

Tessa sang softly while she played—a beautiful,

soothing song—and as I listened, my paintbrush moved more easily, too. Art and music hand in hand. Somebody should write a song about that.

Tessa's tune changed, and changed again. Eventually I realized that an hour or more had passed. I stepped back and looked at my painting.

*Don't overwork it,* I could imagine Mimi saying. *Stop before you think you're done.*

I put down my brush and took off my smock.

"Hurray!" Tessa said, strumming a quick fanfare on the guitar. "You did it!"

"Do you like it?" I asked.

Tessa came and looked. I waited, feeling my heart patter a little.

"It's beautiful," she said finally. "It doesn't look like a kid's picture. You know? It's . . . a real painting. Anybody would be glad to have it, not just somebody who loves you."

I understood what she meant. When we were little, our moms had put our art on the refrigerator just because it was ours. Now, with this painting, I had moved past that.

"Thanks," I said. "Your songs were beautiful, too, Tessa."

A car pulled into the driveway, and Tessa

looked out the window. "That's my mom," she said. "I've got to go now."

As I watched Tessa leave, I felt a pang of sadness, wondering when we'd hang out together again. Having her at the ranch had felt almost like the old days, but different. She hadn't painted with me, like she used to, but she'd brought her music into the studio, and that was nice, too. That gave me hope that maybe we could still find ways to do the things we loved—together.

On Wednesday, Gabi and I rehearsed the Professor Picasso Show—in the rain. Thursday was wet and dreary, too. People think we never have to worry about the weather in Albuquerque, but it *does* rain. Farmers were happy, but everybody planning the fiesta—including me—was freaking out.

I was also freaking out about leading the parade on Picasso. After school on Thursday, Luis and I tried to practice the parade gait with Picasso. He would take a few high steps for me, but then he'd fall back into his regular jog. He seemed sluggish and depressed, and by the end of the hour, so was I.

"Don't give up on him," said Luis as we walked

Picasso back toward the shed. "He's a parade horse. When he's in front of the crowd, he'll perform—you wait and see."

I hoped more than anything that Luis was right.

That night after dinner, Gabi and Carmen came over to help Mom and me bake some *biscochitos* for the bake sale. While we rolled out dough and cut out circle shapes, Mom placed the cookies on baking sheets and dusted them with sugar and cinnamon.

"You know," Gabi said thoughtfully, "when we had a bake sale for the animal shelter, we got more money if we said the food was 'free with a donation.'"

"Really?" Carmen asked.

"Sure," Gabi said. "If you say a cookie is fifty cents, that's what people give you. If you ask for a donation, lots of times they give more."

I turned to Mom. "Should we try that?" I asked.

"I'll see what the other PTA members think," Mom said, "but it sounds like a very smart idea."

While the cookies baked in the oven, we helped Dad with the balloon-ticket booth. It took lots of hands to stretch the bright, colorful silk over the wires. It looked great when it was done, like a miniature hot-air balloon.

## Painter's Block

Staring at that beautiful balloon, I felt my hopes for the fiesta lift off the ground. We had worked so hard. The fiesta was going to be a success—it had to be!

But that night, I lay awake listening to the wind in the cottonwoods outside my window. It still sounded like rain. With each passing moment, another "What if?" crossed my mind. *What if it rains on Saturday? What if no one comes out for the fiesta? What if everyone comes out, but I can't get Picasso to do the parade gait? What if I embarrass myself in front of everybody?* And worse yet, *What if I let Mimi down?*

It *didn't* rain on Saturday. After a restless sleep, I woke to pale dawn light at my window. I leaped out of bed and ran to look out. There wasn't a single cloud in the sky. Hurrah!

Mom made me eat breakfast, even though I wasn't hungry. Then we packed up the truck and set off toward the park, where Luis and Picasso were already waiting. Picasso was eating hay from a net hung on the outside of the horse trailer.

As soon as I saw Picasso, I felt a swell of panic. The parade was just minutes away, and I would be leading it—on a horse who *didn't* want to do his parade gait for me. I suddenly felt sick.

Luckily, there was a lot going on to distract me. We were surrounded by other horses, mules, burros, and an enormous team of oxen pulling a huge *carreta*, or cart with wooden wheels. I could hear a band practicing, and I caught sight of Tessa and her music friends unrolling a banner that read *Music Rocks!* Mimi's friend Celeste, who was in charge of the fiesta, bustled around telling everyone what to do.

As I brushed Picasso's long silver forelock, my nerves spiraled out of control again. "Are you going to help me make Mimi proud today?" I asked him. "Please?"

Picasso just looked back at me, his eyes perfectly calm. Was he *too* calm?

I decided to warm him up a little. I saddled, bridled, and mounted him and then rode around the parking lot near where Luis was working. Picasso's strides were long and smooth—lovely to ride, but nothing like his parade gait. Before I could practice that, I heard Celeste call everyone to attention.

"Line up," she bellowed. "Line up!"

As Picasso and I rode to the head of the parade line, butterflies took flight in my stomach. I glanced toward Luis, who gave me a nod and an encouraging smile. Slowly the other horses and riders, oxen, and marchers lined up behind us. Finally, Celeste waved me forward.

*Okay, how do I do this again?* an anxious little voice asked in my head. I made myself tall, sat deep in the saddle, and gave Tessa's earrings a tiny shake to make them jingle. But Picasso simply jogged.

*Please, Picasso,* I begged him silently. *Please do it for Mimi.*

Nothing happened. For a moment, time stood still, and all I could see was Mimi's face—tan and vibrant, the way she'd looked in the ring the day she taught me how to parade ride.

*Lift the reins,* I could almost hear Mimi saying.

I brought the reins up to mid-chest level, letting my free hand hang at my side. That brought my body into that magical alignment, and I felt Picasso change beneath me. A gasp came from someone in the crowd as Picasso arched his neck and began prancing. He was doing it!

We led the parade out of the parking lot and down the blocked-off street. People lined the sidewalks, cheering when we came into sight. That made Picasso prance even more.

*Fire and feather.*

I could tell how impressive Picasso was. He seemed so powerful and high-spirited, some people edged back as we passed. Only I could tell how calm he was underneath it all. He was loving this! And I was, too.

Ahead of us the bright sun gleamed off the chrome of a wheelchair. Wait, it couldn't be . . .

Oh yes, it could! It was Mimi, wearing her big hat and her big white smile, a smile I hadn't seen in a very long time. I wanted to ride straight to her and fall off into her arms. Picasso swiveled his ears toward Mimi. He wanted to go to her, too.

"Not yet," I whispered to him. "First, let's

make Mimi proud." I sat tall and waved at Mimi. She waved back.

Picasso and I continued our circuit through the neighborhood. The streets were lined with cheering people all along the way. After turning one corner and then another, we finally arrived back at the little park where the parade ended and the fiesta began.

As I dismounted and led Picasso toward the trailer, I saw Dad's balloon-ticket booth, the PTA bake-sale table, the barbecue pit already starting to smoke, and all the artists' booths. Everyone working at the tables and booths clapped for us, too. It made a good grand finale.

In the far corner of the park, Luis waited near the trailer. "You did it, Saige," he said as he helped me unsaddle Picasso. "You made your grandma very proud and happy."

Hearing Luis's words, all I wanted to do was go find Mimi, but there was still so much more to do!

Gabi was waiting for me inside the horse trailer, where we changed into our Lovely Assistant costumes—long black skirts with royal blue T-shirts that matched Picasso's Thinking Cap. We had dyed the cap and painted glittery spirals and stars onto the ears. It looked awesome!

We could hear the other acts getting started. The acrobats had the stage first, and then Tessa's singing group. I could hear their first song from inside the trailer, and I was impressed. They were really good.

Then someone started a solo. Her voice was so strong and pure that I had to step outside the trailer to see who it was. *Tessa*.

I'd never heard Tessa sound quite like this. Was the inside of her mouth like a cathedral? Were her jaw hinges made of rubber? I had no idea. I just heard her voice, big and full and beautiful. I wanted to run onstage and announce, "That's *my* best friend singing!"

And suddenly, I understood—Tessa *had* to do this. She had to sing, and sing well, and sing as often as she could.

"Amazing!" I heard Gabi say from over my shoulder. "You and Tessa are both so talented. It's no wonder that you're friends."

Gabi was right. My friendship with Tessa made sense somehow. For just a moment, I imagined us as grown-ups, Tessa coming to my gallery openings and me going to her concerts. We'd have other friends, but we'd always understand each other in a special way . . . wouldn't we? Watching her sing, I felt a flutter of sadness over all we'd been through in the last few weeks, but it was mingled with something else—hope, maybe.

I clapped extra hard when Tessa took her bow, and then Gabi nudged me. It was our turn.

Gabi and I adjusted Picasso's Thinking Cap on his ears and then led him onstage. I glanced out at the crowd—and did a double take when I saw Mom pushing Mimi into the front row. Mimi winked at me, and I grinned back. I couldn't believe this moment was finally here!

Celeste handed Gabi the portable microphone. For a second, Gabi looked pale and scared. She flicked on the microphone and said, "Testing, testing."

I knew how nervous Gabi felt. I had felt the same way just minutes ago at the start of the parade. She needed my help, so I did the only thing I could think of: when she looked my way, I imitated Picasso's "duh" face. That made her smile, and the color came back to her cheeks.

Gabi cleared her throat and said, "I'd like to introduce Professor Picasso. Professor, will you take a bow, please?"

We'd taught Picasso to stretch down like a dog,

reaching his front legs forward and lowering his chest toward the ground. We curtseyed at the same time. Everyone cheered, and under the cover of the sound, I clicked and gave Picasso a treat.

"Professor Picasso will do a painting first," Gabi explained. "And then he will take questions from the audience. Professor, are you ready?"

I pointed my index finger at Picasso's chest. His ears snapped forward, and he nodded sharply. Everyone gasped, and Gabi grinned at me. We had our audience in the palms of our hands.

I set up his table and pad, and Picasso, working with his back to the audience, applied his traditional three colors. He produced a handsome abstract piece, mostly blue. The audience applauded. When I saw the huge grin on Mimi's face, I felt my chest nearly *burst* with pride and happiness. But the act wasn't over yet. I forced myself to stay focused on Picasso.

I shortened the lead rope to stop Picasso from kissing his painting, something he still liked to do. Gabi carefully tore the painting off the pad and handed it to Celeste.

"Be sure to bid on Picasso's latest masterpiece over at the silent auction," Gabi told the audience. "Now Professor Picasso will answer some questions."

I turned him to face the crowd. The audience went very still.

"First, Picasso," Gabi said, "are you enjoying the fiesta today?"

I pointed my finger at Picasso's shoulder, and he nodded. *Yes.*

"Are you a supporter of arts in school?"

*Yes.*

"Do you think kids can get a good education *without* arts?"

Picasso shook his head no and stuck his lip up jeeringly. Gabi said, "That means *'Duh!'*" We got a huge laugh out of that one.

"Should the community work to get art and music in every school, every year?" Gabi asked.

I pointed my finger at Picasso's shoulder. He nodded *Yes.* I pointed again and again. *Yes, yes, yes!*

Then Gabi said, "All right, would someone in the audience like to ask a question? It should be something that can be answered with a yes or no."

Hands shot up in the crowd, and Gabi pointed at people one by one, taking their questions.

"Did you have fun leading the parade?"

*Yes.*

"Will Oakland win the World Series?"

I went for *Duh* on that one.

A little girl stood up, took her thumb out of her mouth, and asked Picasso, "Can you *talk*?"

She really believed in Picasso, and I knew I had to be careful. I gave Picasso the *Yes* signal and then said to the girl, "Every horse can talk. Horses may not talk the way *we* do, but we can learn to hear them." The little girl's eyes widened, and I could tell she was listening hard.

Now Mimi raised her left hand. "Picasso, are you glad to see me?" she asked.

Picasso's ears leaped forward at the familiar sound of her voice. He was done with the show now. Quietly, calmly, he towed me over to Mimi and bent his head to sniff her face. Nobody clapped, but a sound went up from the audience, a long "oooh." It was the perfect finale. Gabi took her bows and came to join us.

Mimi stroked Picasso's long white nose with her left hand and kissed him. His blue, starry ears pointed peacefully out to the sides. I could tell he'd been wondering for the past two weeks, *Where is Mimi? Is she ever coming back?* They both looked so happy that I didn't want to interrupt.

Too soon, though, Gabi and I had to lead

## The Fiesta

Picasso away with a gentle tug on the halter rope.
I helped Luis load Picasso onto the trailer, and then
I went back to talk to Mimi.

When she saw me, Mimi squeezed my hand
with her good one. "That was *wonderful!*" she said.
"I'm so proud of all three of you."

I was so happy that I felt as if I were floating.
"I still have a drawing lesson to teach," I told Mimi.
"Gabi's going to teach kids how to draw dogs, and
I'm going to teach them how to draw horses—just
like you taught me." I could still remember Mimi
holding my hand in hers, guiding my pencil as
I drew.

Mimi smiled and squeezed my hand again.
"That reminds me," she said. "I have a present for
you." She pulled a sheet of paper out of the bag in
her lap.

It was a drawing of Picasso—a wobbly,
wavering, all-over-the-place ink drawing that
perfectly captured his gentlemanly yet fiery spirit.
Even the dribbles and blots fell in all the right places.
It was different from anything Mimi had ever done.

I sucked in my breath. "Mimi, it's amazing!"
I finally said.

"Isn't it?" she said. "I did it with my left hand,

thanks to your idea—and the felt-tipped brush-pen. I've never done anything this loose and free. It's exactly the style I've been looking for. It . . . it makes me want to kick up my heels like a filly!"

Mimi flashed a smile—her real smile—and I felt my throat tighten with emotion. Mimi still looked pale and small in her wheelchair, but when I saw that smile, I knew that she was going to be okay.

The drawing lesson flew by, and then the fiesta was suddenly, amazingly, over. After all that preparation, it seemed so short—fun and wonderful, but short. It looked as if it had been successful, too. No cookies were left, and Mom said Gabi's idea about donations had worked well. "Some people paid ten dollars for two *biscochitos*," she said, "or twenty-five dollars for a peach pie!"

The works of art in the silent auction had long lists of bids. My painting had several bids, which made me proud. Picasso's painting had the most, though. He commanded a higher price even than Mimi's saddle painting. "It's hard to compete with a Picasso, Mimi!" I told her.

Dad's Stetson hat was full of raffle-ticket stubs,

and the cash box was full of money. We didn't even know how much yet.

"You did a great job today, Saige," Mom said as we packed the balloon booth into the pickup truck. "You kids really earned your art class, and I think you showed the community how much art matters— to all of us."

"Even to horses!" I said. Then I yawned hugely. I'd never felt so tired.

Monday morning, Dad drove Gabi and me to school at the crack of dawn. We carried in the stack of drawings from the fiesta. A few janitors were walking around, along with Mrs. Applegate, who had agreed to meet us. She helped us find step stools and masking tape, and we hung the drawings—dog pictures on one side of the hall and horses on the other. Above each group we put a sign that read "Created at the Fiesta to Support Arts Education."

When we were done, Gabi and I stood back to look. "I can't wait to see how people like our drawings," she said excitedly.

"Me, neither," I murmured, taking it all in.

My mind flashed back to the first day of school,

which seemed so long ago now. I remembered walking down that long beige hall, not knowing yet that there would be no art class this year. Not knowing that things had changed between Tessa and me. Not knowing Gabi at all.

We still didn't have an art class at school, and I didn't know if my friendship with Tessa would ever be the same again. But I had Gabi. And those blank, beige walls were suddenly alive with art. Some horses were shaped like dachshunds and some dogs were shaped like horses. There were a few really realistic-looking dogs and horses, too. The pictures did what pictures always do—they made me want to draw.

As Gabi and I walked into our empty classroom, I pulled out a single piece of blank white paper from my backpack. I smoothed it out on the table in front of me and sat down. Then I got out my felt-tipped brush-pen, balanced it in my hand—my left hand—thought about Picasso, and began to draw.

# Letter from American Girl

Dear Readers,

After Mimi is injured, Saige has to rely on her imagination and creative "workarounds" to keep the arts fund-raiser on track. She trains Mimi's beloved old horse Picasso how to do new tricks and learns that she, Picasso, and her friend Gabi make a great team.

Here's the story of a real girl who loves horses just as much as Saige does. She teaches her pony Toby how to do tricks—and even how to give hugs! Like Saige, this determined girl doesn't let life's challenges stand in the way of pursuing her passion. We hope her story will inspire you.

Your friends at American Girl

# Lizzy's Ride

I've been around horses my whole life. My parents breed and train show horses, and we live on a farm in Pennsylvania with green fields, white fences, and miles of riding trails. My parents put me on horseback before I could even walk. You might be surprised to learn that I wasn't always horse crazy. Until I was about seven, I was more interested in soccer and art.

Around that time, something changed. As I got to know each of our horses, I got more attached to them. Horses are like people. They have so much personality. And just as some people click with each other, the same thing happens with people and horses. For me and my pony Toby, that's definitely true. We're similar because we both know what it's like to be underestimated.

See, I was born with only one hand. That might seem like a big deal, but it's really not. I've been this way my whole life. Everyone faces challenges, and this one is mine. But I have never let it get in my way. I know that if I work hard, I can do everything that people think I can't do.

Just as some people think less of a 12-year-old girl with one hand, they think an unwanted pony isn't worth much, either. My mom bought Toby at a horse auction. Who knows where he might have ended up if she hadn't found him. He was for sale with a bunch of other scared, homeless horses. From inside a stall, he kicked over a bucket and stepped up on it, like he was doing whatever he could to say to my mom, "Pick me! Pick me!" My parents brought him home the next day, and he became my first show pony. A lot of people thought of Toby as just a common auction pony, but I knew he could be great. Together, we make a great team.

Quiet time in the barn

Silly pony!

119

Jumps are more challenging without a saddle or bridle— it's harder to hang on.

Toby has taught me a lot about horsemanship and riding. He's also taught me about compassion and solving problems. He was the first pony I ever cantered or jumped, but he was also the first to dump me in the dirt. If he were a person, he'd be that funny kid at school who always seems to get away with breaking rules—but everyone loves him anyway.

Working with Toby, I've figured out that if I'm cranky with a horse, he'll be cranky right back. I've learned that when I treat a horse the way I want him to treat me, we seem to understand each other better—like what happens with friends. Because of Toby, I am softer and kinder in almost everything I do.

A few years ago, a well-known stunt rider invited me and some of our horses to join his show. Since then, I have taught Toby and my other pony, Puddles, cues for tricks such as "bow," "lie down," "stand on a box," and even "jump through fire." Sometimes as part of a performance, we jump a course of small obstacles without using a saddle or a bridle—I guide the pony with just a thin neck loop decorated with flowers. When we finish, the ponies get lots of praise, kisses, treats, and applause. I've also been working on a new trick that I call "the hug." In this trick, Toby wraps his front hoof around my foot and then bends his neck around to hug me. For our tricks to work, we have to trust each other. And we do.

Twice a month during the school year and more often during the summer, my family and I pack up the horses and hit the road, driving to the horse shows and events where we perform. Last fall, I performed every day for more than two weeks at a horse event in Kentucky.

Ta-da! Take a bow, Toby.

My grandma came along to tutor me and make sure I didn't get behind on schoolwork. The best part about performing is sharing what my horses and I have worked on so hard.

I'll keep working hard. I'm competing in horse shows, and I exercise four to six horses a day. I'm also busy with barn chores such as cleaning stalls and picking up rocks in the field. And one day, I hope to join an American equestrian team and compete internationally.

Together we ride like the wind.

Up and over!

I have a belief about life: dream big, and don't ever let anything get in the way of making your dreams come true. Even small dreams can mean a lot—like wishing that one of my performances will bring a smile to someone's face or just hoping that my once-homeless pony will run over to me when he sees me at the gate. It's a little thing, but I can't even describe how great it feels.

Jessie Haas grew up loving horses, drawing horses, riding horses, and reading every horse book she could find—so it's no wonder that when she began writing, most of her 36 books turned out to be about horses. She's written picture books, easy readers, historical novels, poetry, and nonfiction. Many of her books have won awards, including *Horse Crazy, Chase,* and *Jigsaw Pony.*

Jessie has always trained her own horses, a job made easier and more fun when she discovered clicker training. She also loves to knit, cook, and read.

Jessie lives in a solar-powered cabin next door to the Vermont farm she grew up on. She shares her home with her husband, Michael J. Daley (also a children's book author), two cats, a dog, and an adventurous hen. Her brave and opinionated Morgan horse, Robin, lives on the family farm, along with a small herd of Irish Dexters, a rare breed of cattle.